"So you're not a reporter?" Justin asked.

A vast uneasiness swept through Kristin. She *was* a reporter. But it was clear that she couldn't admit it. She might find herself back in the snow.

"I swear to you, I don't know what you're talking about." There, she hadn't lied.

"I never told you not to come here?"

"I would never have asked you if I could come here!" she snapped. "I don't need your permission to travel on public roads." A soft flush covered her cheeks. "I don't know who you think was coming here for what, but it wouldn't be worth it! Nothing would be worth it!"

"Not even one of the hottest scoops of the decade?" Justin suggested politely.

"Not even that," Kristin assured him sweetly.

Was it the truth? Despite herself—and him—Kristin was growing intrigued.

D1014044

Dear Reader,

I have several very exciting things to talk about this month; in fact, it's hard to know where to begin. How about with a piece of news some of you have been waiting years to hear?

In 1986, Kristin James wrote a novel for Silhouette Intimate Moments called *A Very Special Favor.* The hero of that book had two brothers, and over the years, I've received quite a lot of letters asking for their stories. This month, I'm glad to oblige with *Salt of the Earth,* the first step in completing THE MARSHALLS, a family-based trilogy. In August look for *The Letter of the Law,* to complete the series. And here's another piece of terrific news: anyone who missed *A Very Special Favor* the first time around will get a second chance to purchase it this fall, as part of a special in-store promotion. Look for it in your bookstores.

If that's not enough excitement for you, here's more: Kay Hooper is back with *The Haviland Touch,* a sequel to her first—and very popular—Intimate Moments novel, *Enemy Mine.* Of course, this suspenseful and adventure-filled story stands on its own, so whether you've read that first book or not, you have a treat in store this month.

Round out the month with Heather Graham Pozzessere's *Snowfire,* a nice wintry story to balance the summer heat, and Marilyn Tracy's *Echoes of the Garden,* in which long-estranged lovers are brought together by their love for their son. In coming months, look for books by Nora Roberts, Linda Howard, Kathleen Eagle, Naomi Horton, Emilie Richards and all of the other wonderful authors who make Silhouette Intimate Moments one of the most exciting series in romance fiction today.

Leslie Wainger
Senior Editor and
Editorial Coordinator

HEATHER GRAHAM POZZESSERE

Snowfire

SILHOUETTE·INTIMATE·MOMENTS®

Published by Silhouette Books New York

America's Publisher of Contemporary Romance

SILHOUETTE BOOKS
300 East 42nd St., New York, N.Y. 10017

SNOWFIRE

Copyright © 1991 by Heather Graham Pozzessere

All rights reserved. Except for use in any review,
the reproduction or utilization of this work in
whole or in part in any form by any electronic,
mechanical or other means, now known or
hereafter invented, including xerography,
photocopying and recording, or in any information
storage or retrieval system, is forbidden without
the permission of the publisher, Silhouette Books,
300 E. 42nd St., New York, N.Y. 10017

ISBN: 0-373-07386-0

First Silhouette Books printing June 1991

All the characters in this book are fictitious. Any
resemblance to actual persons, living or dead, is
purely coincidental.

®: Trademark used under license and
registered in the United States Patent and
Trademark Office and in other countries.

Printed in the U.S.A.

HEATHER GRAHAM POZZESSERE

considers herself lucky to live in Florida, where she can indulge her love of water sports, such as swimming and boating, year round. Her background includes stints as a model, actress and a bartender. She was once actually tied to the railroad tracks to garner publicity for the dinner theater where she was acting. Now she's a full-time wife, mother of five and, of course, a writer of historical and contemporary romances.

This one is for
Cousin G—A.K.A.
Auntie Tomato—A.K.A.
Cousin-Kiss-of-Death—A.K.A.
Miss Gail Astrella—
with lots of love
and many thanks for all the
best of times

Prologue

Looking out the window, Justin could see the moonlight on the snow. It dazzled, it shimmered, it flickered like fire, as if the cold could burn.

Snow fire. *Snowfire*.

As beautiful and as treacherous as the people involved in his new play. *Snowfire*. Aptly named.

"Justin!"

The call was soft. Sensual. Justin knew that when he turned, Myra would be standing in the doorway to his study.

He'd come to the study to be alone. To escape Myra and her endless party. But she had followed him. He didn't need to turn to know that her lashes would be cast low over her cheeks and that she'd have a breathless appearance, as if she were longing to see him.

Myra was always the actress, even when she was off the stage.

He stiffened his back, rubbing the back of his neck without turning. "What is it, Myra?"

"Artie says you're not coming back to New York."

Justin looked back out at the snow, at the beautiful, crystalline snow. He wished Myra would leave him in peace.

But Myra wasn't in the mood for peace. She was never in the mood for peace.

Justin walked around his desk and sat in his chair, looking at her at last. She was just as he had imagined her—seductive, enchanting, artificial. Her dress had a high slit along the thigh and she was standing so that the fabric would fall away, revealing a long expanse of leg. Her blue eyes were large and wide, and she kept her hair a sunlit blond. It was long, draping over her shoulder elegantly.

He put all of these pieces together and reminded himself that she was still as beautiful as he had once thought her. Funny. It was hard for him to find that beauty now. The softness of her voice did nothing to arouse him. The only thing that could affect him now was when he saw fear enter her eyes. She was such a child. She used him, she abused him, but he didn't hate her. He pitied her. She was so afraid of the future. Afraid of aging, of losing the adoration of the masses. And once, once he had thought that he loved her. He felt responsible. She was still his wife, even if he was growing more and more anxious for the marriage to end.

"Artie is right," he told her, leaning back. "I'm not coming back to New York."

She pouted. It was a practiced pout. It might have seeped its way into many a man's heart. Justin merely smiled. He knew her too well.

She walked over and sat on the corner of his desk. A provocative pose once again. It just didn't work anymore. "Justin," she purred. She reached over to fluff his hair. "Hey, tall, dark and handsome! You have to come back. I'll make it worth your while."

For a brief moment, he felt a curious hesitation. He had married her. Once, he had thought her every bit as beautiful and passionate and incredible as the rest of the world did. And she had seen something in him. She had been equally attracted. She liked tall men, she liked broad shoulders. Woodsy men—even if she hated the woods.

He had thought that he loved her, and in a reckless moment he had married her. He had always thought that when he married, it would be forever, that he would respect his vows. And Myra almost sounded now as if she still wanted it to work. As if she would try. Really try.

I don't love you anymore, he thought. But maybe love could be regained. No. Myra wasn't made for marriage. Not with him, anyway. He had believed in a certain commitment to each other, and God only knew just how many times Myra had betrayed him, with just how many men. There were even rumors out now that she was sleeping with her two male costars in *Snowfire,* the play he had written for her when she begged him to help her get her career back on track.

Justin smiled. He found that one unlikely. Jack Jones was young and handsome, the perfect hero, but in real life he was not picky about which sex he chose for his affairs. And Harry Johnston, while he was a wonderful character actor, a man who had once stolen the respect and admiration of a nation, had such a severe case of alcoholism that producers and directors had been blackballing him. Just like Myra, Harry had come to him for help. And Justin had begged the director of *Snowfire* to give Harry a chance. Everybody deserved a second chance. Justin just hoped Harry would continue to do well, for he knew the director had threatened that if Harry took even one drink, he would be out of the play.

Justin sighed and rubbed his neck again. What a play. Everybody was after something. Jack wanted to prove how masculine he could be. Harry how sober. Myra how beautiful-as-always. And Roxanne, the sweet young ingenue, just wanted to burst her way to stardom. Soft, tiny, delicate—a barracuda! Justin almost smiled anew. Maybe he had been feeling just a little like teaching Myra a lesson when he suggested Roxanne to the play's director. She was everything that Myra wanted to regain—she was very, very young.

And they were all in his house right now. Not his New York penthouse, but his real home, his place in the New England countryside. Myra had invited them all. *Snowfire* had opened to rave reviews and was already a huge commercial success. So tonight, on their Monday "black" day, they had all chartered a small plane and flown here. They had done nothing but party since they arrived.

Justin frowned as a puzzling thought hit him. Myra hated the house. But Myra had invited them all. The film critic and his wife. Christina—his own agent. And Artie Fein, poor, ever-worried little Artie, Myra's agent. And the cast of *Snowfire*. The boozer, the swinger, the schemer—and the whore, he thought wearily, that being, of course, his own wife.

But who was he to judge them? he asked himself in fairness. No one. He was bitter tonight. Because it was all for show and he wanted more.

He wanted the house to be a home. He wanted . . .

What did he want?

He didn't know. Yes, he did. He wanted to look into a woman's eyes and see warmth instead of calculation. He wanted love, and most of all, he wanted trust.

He bore Myra no malice. He just wanted out.

She was leaning toward him, her eyes very wide. And her dress, of course, was gaping at the breast.

"Justin . . . ?" That soft, soft, slinky whisper.

He smiled broadly, shaking his head. He stared at her with steady eyes, eyes so dark blue that they seemed cobalt or black at times. Times like this.

"Sorry, Myra. I have made my decision. I'm not coming back."

Her voice changed quickly. "Damn you, Justin. You have to come back. Your name is everywhere—"

"Whoa, whoa!" he told her. "My pseudonym is everywhere right now, Myra. But your name is out there, too." He leaned forward. "Myra, let's face it. What's left of our marriage? You moved out on me, you slept with everything with two legs in Hollywood, you did that awful movie, and—"

"I did not sleep with everything with legs!"

He cast her a narrow-eyed glance and she had the good grace to flush.

"I'll make it up to you. I won't ever run around again. I'll—"

"I know you told me you wanted to come back to me, but will you live out here?" he asked her softly. "Just part-time? Will you slow down? Will you have a baby?"

"What!" Those wide, wide eyes of hers were on him. Then she tried to cover her dismay. "Sure, Justin, sure. Soon. I couldn't possibly do so right now, though. I have to get my career on track, I have to—"

"Myra," he interrupted her softly. "I have to get my life on track. I wrote you a play, Myra—you're starring in it, it's magnificent, you're magnificent. Now it's my turn. I'm starting the legal proceedings tomorrow—"

"No! I won't let you. Justin, I need you!"

"You don't need me!" he snapped. He was losing it. "You think you need my name! And you think you need my arm for a publicity photo here and there."

Myra jumped off his desk. "You're a bastard, Justin. I need at least a year! Then I'll be successful enough again. Give me that!"

"Myra, I'll give you until tomorrow morning to get out of this house, that's what I'll give you now."

"Oh!" In a sudden whirl of fury, she threw herself against him.

Myra was strong, quick and obsessed. Justin didn't want to hurt her, but she had mile-long nails and she was quick to try to gouge his face. He found her shoulders and thrust her away from him. She slammed back against the door frame.

"Stop it!" he warned her, shaking. There was a trickle of blood oozing from his lip. He wiped it with the back of his hand.

"You'll pay, Justin," she promised. She was raging with fury, not a tear in her eyes. There was not a weak thing about her. But when Artie Fein came running, she suddenly seemed about to fall.

Artie caught her. "Hey, hey!" he said, his eyes darting from Justin to Myra and back again. "What's going on here?"

Myra burst into tears. As if from a faucet, water just sprang to her eyes, making them luminous. "Oh!" she wailed. "Oh, how could you!" Her voice seemed to carry throughout the entire house.

And suddenly the hallway, and his office—his little haven—were full. Jack Jones, blond and handsome but just a little too soft-looking; Roxanne, delicate and tough.

"What the hell is going on here?" Roxanne demanded. She looked at Myra suspiciously.

"Good Lord!" boomed Harry Johnston. He held his hand in his jacket, just like Napoleon.

Christina, always quiet, smooth and watchful, appeared behind Harry. "What's going on?" she asked.

"Nothing—" Justin began irritably, but Myra had her audience now, and she was onstage.

"It's Justin, he's being so horrible to me. He—he threatened to kill me."

"Oh, the hell I did!" Justin roared. His anger seemed to stab at his temples like a knife. "Myra, get out. Just get the hell out!"

She turned, wrenching herself from Artie's arms. Everyone stared awkwardly at Justin.

There was a big thud followed by an anguished whining. Justin's lips tightened grimly, and he felt his face whiten with his anger.

Myra. Damn her. She hated Jugs, his hound-mixture puppy, as much as she hated the house. And it sounded as if she had just kicked him out of her way.

Enough. Justin strode through the crowd gathered around his office and out to the living room, where the fire burned.

It was a lovely room. His favorite. Glass doors led out to a glass-enclosed pool. The room was fashioned of granite and brick and wood, and though very contemporary, it was also amazingly warm and comfortable. Beyond the glass the water rippled in a beautiful aqua shade. The night sky was velvet-black. The snow was an almost unearthly white.

But Myra was there, marring the picture. She was gloating as she stared at him. She'd hurt his dog—she'd hurt him at last. He tried to understand.

Hell, he just tried to control his temper.

But he'd done everything he could for her. He'd forgiven her the lovers, the drinking, the drugs. He'd picked her up, and he'd done his best to put her back on her feet. But she wasn't done with him yet. She didn't want him, but she couldn't bear the fact that he was really done with her before she had finished with him.

Jugs, huddled over by the glass doors to the pool, nervously wagged his tail. The film critic, Joseph Banks, gray-haired, ever pleasant, sat on the couch with his equally charming and pleasant wife. Both were staring at him uncomfortably.

Justin didn't care.

He gripped Myra's shoulders. "It's over, don't you understand? It's over! And if you ever hurt that poor dog again, well, hell, Myra, maybe I will just strangle you!"

He let go of her shoulders because his hands were so taut he really might have snapped her collarbones. He turned swiftly, realizing that Banks was still watching him. With pity.

"I'm sorry, Joseph," Justin began. He opened his mouth to speak again, but he just didn't have anything to say. "I'm sorry—oh, hell!"

He walked through to the entryway, grabbed an overcoat from the hall coat tree and plunged out into the snow.

The cold outside embraced him. Wrapped around him. Numbed him. It felt good. It felt so damned good.

He walked down the long driveway to the road. It was a good distance, especially in the snow. When he reached the road, he looked around. There was nothing out there. Just silence. The nearest house was miles away. He liked the solitude. He liked his neighbors well enough—they liked the solitude, too.

It was just Myra....

He looked up at the moon. I tried! he explained, as if he were praying. Lord, you know that I tried. I did everything I could for her.

There was no answer. Or maybe there was. The snow had made him feel more peaceful.

He and Myra had to solve their own problems. Meanwhile there was a party going on—he had guests. He turned and started back to the house.

But while he'd been thinking, he had wandered down the slope of the hill near the house, and so he trudged across the yard and approached the house from the back. The snow was high, almost to his knees.

On the path between the garage and the main building, he paused suddenly. An unease began to creep along his spine.

There was something in the snow. Something lying there, highlighted by the lights of the garage. Marring the purity of the white...

He was frozen for a moment, and then he started to run.

It was a body that marred the snow. A woman's body. Myra's body.

''Myra!''

He ran as he shouted, and he fell to his knees beside her, sweeping her up.

She was coatless and hatless, wearing nothing but her evening dress....

And her long red scarf.

The scarf was wound tightly around her neck. He struggled to loosen it. She was white, chalk white. Except where a trace of blue showed.

Because she was dead.

His fingers ceased their frantic struggle with the scarf. Myra was dead.

"My God," he whispered aloud. Sorrow filled him. He no longer loved her, had often been furious with her. But he had cared about her still. And he was sorry, too, for the waste of life and beauty and for dreams gone so very far awry. He cradled her in his arms.

"Justin!" someone wailed.

Jack Jones, in his overcoat, was behind him. And Harry was behind Jack. Christina and Roxanne were hurrying out, their coats all bundled around them.

"Oh, my Lord!" Roxanne screamed.

"You've killed her!" Artie wailed. "Justin, you've gone and killed her!"

"No! Hell, no! I didn't kill her, I just found her!" Justin protested.

Then he looked at the faces around him. And he looked down at Myra. Someone had killed her. Poor, bedeviled Myra. His marriage was over at last.

And as she had said . . . he certainly was going to pay.

He closed his eyes, holding the cold form of his dead wife. She would never know just how ironic her words were going to prove to be. Long before he heard the shrill of the sirens, he knew that indeed, he was going to pay.

Chapter 1

Five Years Later

"Snow flurries!"

Kristin said the words aloud in absolute disgust. She was nearly blinded by the heavy flakes obscuring the road ahead. Nervously she released the grip of one hand from the wheel of the car to toss back a thick lock of rich dark hair over her shoulders. She narrowed dove-gray eyes, grown silver with her apprehension, and concentrated fully upon the road—or lack thereof—once again.

The weatherman in Boston had predicted snow flurries for the weekend, but Kristin didn't think this heavy precipitation could be called flurries by any stretch of the imagination. Within thirty minutes the sky had gone from silver-gray to a deep dark charcoal, and large snowflakes were falling in a frenzy on her red Cherokee.

And it was too late to turn back. Far too late. She wasn't sure she could turn around if she tried. She wasn't even sure that she was still on the right road. Or on any road at all, as a matter of fact. Not that she didn't know her way—she did. She'd driven out here to the country to visit Roger and Sue several times.

But she'd never done so in the snow before. And this section of the state was isolated at the best of times. The nights could be black, pitch-black. And now with the storm . . .

Was she lost? She didn't even know the answer to that! This was a remote area, with very few houses. Creeping along as slowly as she had to, she hadn't seen a house in ages. She was barely moving, at three to five miles an hour, and even then she was afraid that she was going to swerve into an awful slide at any moment. If she were just on I-495 or the Mass Pike or anything that could be considered a major road, she would stop. Some form of rescue vehicle would eventually come for her. But she wasn't. There were no major roads out here. She couldn't stop. No one else might pass by for days.

She was afraid to stop. New England, for all the horrid reputation of its weather, hadn't had a winter like this in years. Yet Kristin could still remember the blizzard that had struck so suddenly some years ago, leaving commuters stranded, and hundreds of drivers caught in the snow. It had been tragic. People had literally frozen to death in their cars.

Despite the fine heating system in her Cherokee, Kristin shivered at the thought. She'd written an article on that blizzard. She had interviewed people who made it to hospitals in varying stages of hypothermia, and the workers who dug out the ones that had died.

''Flurries!'' she snarled out loud again—for courage, for a sense of having company with whom to share the growing fear and misery. She wasn't afraid of flurries;

she had four-wheel drive and great snow tires. She had been driving in the snow since she was sixteen, and she was nearly twenty-eight now. She was competent. Intelligent. She would have never started out in this stinking weather if they had forecast anything worse than flurries. Light flurries at that!

She thought about the weatherman she had watched on the news that morning. "New England, you know," he had teased, certain of his own humor. "If you don't like the weather today, don't worry. It'll change by tomorrow."

Droll, droll . . .

"Flurries, my foot, you fool!" she cried now, exasperated.

Well, this wasn't going to change by tomorrow. These flurries were a full-scale blizzard, and it didn't take a weatherman to know it.

She slowed the car as the wind swept a solid wall of snow into her windshield. As she did so, the car stalled. She sat in stunned and silent disbelief, then shifted into neutral and turned the key again. The starter growled, then the sound faded. Kristin swore vehemently.

She turned the key again, instantly grateful for the chugging she heard, then furious when it, too, died away. She frowned, biting into her lower lip.

Think! Don't panic, she warned herself severely. She leaned forward, narrowing her eyes. Yes! There was a house nearby! Up on the hill above the road. The snow kept trying to conceal it, but when the wind died down for just a second, she could see it! It was set very far back from the road, maybe even five hundred feet. But it was there. And she was almost at the foot of a nearly snow-covered driveway that led to it.

Thank God. All she had to do was knock on the door and call a towing company. Nothing to panic about, nothing at all. If she had veered onto the wrong road, they'd put her back on the right one.

Fighting the wind, she managed to open the car door. The cold wind struck her a buffeting blow, but she braced against it. The weather was getting worse and worse.

She looked up at the house. Well, it wasn't exactly just a house. It was an estate. It was massive, modern, architecturally beautiful. Constructed of wood and stone, it seemed almost a part of the landscape.

Roger had always told her that she would never dream just how many of the rich and the famous built homes out here in the countryside. She'd have to admit that he had been right when she saw him.

If she ever saw him.

The wind was whirling furiously around her. She was afraid she might not even make it to the house if she didn't hurry. She gritted her teeth and started up the driveway.

Whoever lived here out in the middle of nowhere probably didn't like company at all, she thought. But still, surely the maid could let her use a phone!

Resolutely, she pulled her down parka more closely about her, bent her head and hurried up the drive.

Justin had taken a break from his work, a new play called *Whisper of Spring*, just minutes before he saw the woman struggling her way up his driveway.

He cursed. He'd been feeling good, really good, for the first time in a long time. He was working. And that was nice.

He'd tried to work before. But the years had been so bitter and so painful. There'd been the trial—when even his own attorneys hadn't believed in him. There had been the doubt in everyone's eyes. Even Christina, who had professed to believe him, had looked at him differently. His only solace had been here in this house. He had learned to crave privacy and anonymity more than ever before.

And now...

Incredible. The woman was walking up his driveway!

Amazement filled him at first—that anyone, for any reason, would be so foolhardy as to attempt to reach him today.

Then anger swept through him. A fury as blinding as the snow.

Damn her! Damn all reporters! Damn them straight to hell!

Not two hours ago on the telephone, he had warned the reporter from the fledgling magazine not to come. She had insisted that she was going to. He had assured her again and again that he would not see her if she did. She'd tried to tell him that she didn't do sensationalist stories, and he had snarled that he didn't give a damn.

He looked toward the fireplace. Toward the spot where Jugs had once curled up. Well, Jugs wasn't there anymore, and that was thanks to a reporter.

Swearing, he stared out the window again. The reporter was here. And she was probably certain that he'd be forced to let her in because of the weather.

Well, she had another think coming! There was no way she was coming into his house.

No way in hell!

Long before she reached the house, Kristin saw movement.

The door was flung open and a huge man in snow boots and a heavy parka stormed out.

Kristin stopped and assessed him tentatively. He was moving swiftly and with a definite malice.

Though she realized that his parka undoubtedly added bulk and his boots probably made him taller, she could have sworn it was Conan the Barbarian advancing on her.

Here. In this nightmare of endless white and snow...

All she was doing was coming to ask if she could use the phone! she reminded herself. Why did he give her this awful feeling of unease?

He bore down upon her. And he *was* huge, well over six feet. His eyes were like a hawk's, cold as ice, sharp, piercing, angry. They seemed to slam into hers.

"You can get yourself right back into that car!" he thundered.

"I—I—" She was floundering. Absurdly. "My car won't start!" she snapped out with more dignity. "I was coming to phone for help—"

But he had already charged by her. In a second he had jerked open the front door to the Cherokee, and was sliding into the driver's seat.

Kristin hurried back after him. She tried to study the man who now sat in her car. She could see little more than those eyes. A snow cap was pulled low over his brow, and a scarf covered his chin and mouth. It did not cover the violence and vehemence of his voice when he spoke.

"Damn you, I will not accept this kind of a trick, young woman. I told you not to come."

"What?" Kristin gasped in utter astonishment.

"I told you not to come. And you can damn well freeze in the snow before I'll let you anywhere near me! You were warned." His voice was deep, rich. It was also so filled with fury that she felt herself trembling inside.

No, she decided firmly. She wasn't going to cower in front of this half-crazed stranger, even if he was built like a brick wall.

She crunched her way back around the car to the driver's side. "I don't know who the hell you are," she shouted, "and I sure as hell don't want to see you or spend any time with you! My car stalled, and that's it!"

He raised his eyes to heaven in a pointed gesture of annoyance. "You fool! You really will try anything for a scoop, huh?"

He half rose, and his fingers curled around her arm. Long, powerful, leather-gloved. She felt a scream bubbling in her throat. She was alone in the snow. He was going to slit her throat. Rape her, mangle her, leave her body there on the roadway, her blood soaking the white snow...

"Move!"

He practically threw her away from the side of her own car. She went floundering into the snowbank. He didn't even look at her. She staggered up to her feet.

The day just hadn't been going badly enough. She couldn't have just walked up to the house and encountered a nice calm white-aproned maid. Oh, no, she had to run into a brick wall of a maniac. She'd been warned all right. She'd been warned that it was a rough and dangerous world for a woman alone, and that she needed to take care and be smart.

Everybody must have a day for a maniac...

And he was a maniac, all right. But certainly not a rapist. He had released her arm as if she were something so wretched that she might contaminate him through all the thick layers of her clothing and the leather of his gloves.

He had no interest in her, except to get rid of her.

He just didn't understand that the car wouldn't start!

But then, to her total consternation, he had the Cherokee going almost instantly. He revved the engine, then got out, towering over her, though at five feet eight inches, she considered herself rather tall.

"Car trouble, right?" he demanded.

"It had stalled—"

"Now get the hell out of here and don't come back. You were warned. And so help me, God, lady, I'll let you freeze before I'll let you in!"

He turned on his heel and headed back up the driveway toward his house. Amazed, Kristin stared after him, feeling as if her blood boiled within her despite the intense cold all around.

"Hey! Thanks for starting it up!" Kristin called after him.

She didn't expect a response and didn't get one.

"Bastard!" she added, knowing that her voice would not carry against the snow and the growing wind. She blew hard on her gloved hands, then slid back behind the wheel. "Madman!" she muttered. Then she shivered, glad of the warmth of the heater as she closed her door against the elements.

She just wanted to get away as fast as possible. Memories of the sharp piercing fury in the stranger's eyes drove her to step on the gas a bit too hard. The car leaped to life and immediately started to slide. She swore, not allowing herself to brake. The wheel straightened and she set her foot very lightly on the gas.

She had to get to Roger and Sue's as quickly as possible.

She wished that she had told them she would definitely be coming today. But she hadn't known exactly what her plans would be, and she had hated to worry them.

Now she wished that she had worried them. If she had, they would come looking for her when she didn't show up tonight. They would send the cops out...

If they had cops out here.

Of course they did, she chided herself. The highway patrol went everywhere. And she had met that nice bewhiskered old sheriff at Roger's birthday party.

Boy, would she like to see a patrolman now—

The car skidded on a patch of ice. "No!" she cried, feeling it begin to slide wildly across the road. "No, no, no!" she repeated, clutching the wheel and forcing herself not to brake as the Cherokee kept sliding, despite her four-wheel drive and snow tires and the fact that she was doing everything right. She had hit a good-sized patch of ice and that was that. She was spinning. And there was nothing she could do. She was desperately tempted to brake. But that would only make it worse....

She couldn't see a damn thing around her. The snow seemed to be falling in a white blanket now. And on either side of her, the embankment was so high that she might have been on some eternal road to the North Pole and Santa Land.

And the car was completely out of control.

"No, damn it!" she swore out loud.

But it did her no good. The Cherokee plowed deeply into one of those high embankments, and suddenly she was blanketed in white.

Stunned, she stared blindly at the wall ahead of her. The Cherokee's engine made a groaning sound, as if she had wounded it with some malice of intent. Then it went dead.

She yelled at it. How dared the car do such a thing to her? She was careful, she was intelligent, she had taken every precaution!

And the damned car had done this to her anyway.

"See if I defend you to the absolute limit ever again!" she warned the car, slowly, carefully turning her key in the ignition once again. She had to get out of the snowbank.

She was already growing cold. The car had a great heater, but only when the engine was running.

The ignition sputtered, and she began to apologize to the car for calling it names.

But when it continued to sputter without turning over, she started to swear again.

"You start for that absolute maniac and refuse to start for me? What kind of a damn traitor are you?"

The Cherokee had no answer.

She twisted the key again, with no success. All she was doing was grinding the ignition into the ground, she realized. She jerked the key out in sudden fury and threw it onto the seat next to her.

Even as she did so, a creeping feeling of uneasiness began to settle over her. She could die here. These were blizzard conditions. And she was so deep into the country that the Commonwealth of Massachusetts might ignore these roads forever and ever. She was still a good twenty miles from her cousin's house, and she really didn't know the area all that well. Whatever town she was in couldn't possibly boast a population of more than a few hundred, and they would be scattered about over several miles.

There was just her...

And the maniac.

Yes, the maniac.

She looked around. She could see nothing but the embankment and the falling snow, but she hadn't come that far. The maniac's house was back there, somewhere. At least it would be warm there. If the weather were just normal, it wouldn't take that long to walk back.

But it was snowing harder than ever. The wind was wailing at a fever pitch.

"Oh, damn!" she cried out.

In answer, the wind suddenly rose to new heights. A blinding sheet of snow came slamming down onto the car and snowbank alike.

She realized that in another few minutes it might not matter if anyone ever drove by or not. The bright red Cherokee could be totally buried in the snow.

And then she would slowly freeze.

It would begin in her extremities. Her fingers would go, and her toes. Frostbite. Her feet, her hands. Her nose. And then it would become worse. Hypothermia. Thanks to the article she had written on that last big blizzard, she knew exactly how she would die.

At least there would be very little pain....

"Oh, my God, what is the matter with me?" she whispered out loud. She couldn't stay there in the car; it would soon be buried. She had to get out, and she had to make it to that house, no matter how nasty the man who lived there chose to be.

But he wasn't just nasty. He was crazy, she reminded herself.

She pressed against the door. The snow was already piling up outside of it. She almost panicked as she had to push and push against the snow to get the door to open. Finally, it was out far enough so that she could wiggle from her seat and through the opening.

Her feet landed in the snow. She peered through the fury of the stinging flakes. She could just barely make out the lights of the house. It seemed incredibly far away, up on a ridge. She would never reach it, she thought, not with the force of the wind now!

She had to reach it.

Bending her head against the onslaught of the snow, she started trudging back along the road. She slid and tripped in the wet snow, and she had to struggle back to her feet. She kept moving, alarmed by the force of the wind that seemed to push her back even as she pressed forward. She hugged her arms around her chest and plodded on, still bending her head to keep the flakes from blinding her.

It seemed to take forever to go just a few steps. She floundered again, and fell face forward into the snow. Choking, she fought her way back up. She could barely feel her feet already, despite her leather boots and warm wool socks. And her hands...

She tucked them under her arms.

She couldn't feel her nose anymore. She couldn't feel it at all.

She had to reach the house.

He had told her he'd let her freeze before he'd let her near him.

"Oh, who the hell would want to come near you!" she whispered to the wind. He was insane.

But no matter who he thought she was, he wouldn't really allow her to freeze, would he?

Maybe he at least had a barn she could find shelter in. She could reason with him. She could promise not to come near him, not to say a word to him.

He had been so violent, so lethal. . . .

Maybe it would be better simply to die in the snow.

Don't *you* be insane! she warned herself in silence.

She could see the house up to the right. She could see the shape and the outline of it. She could see the lights through the window.

She came to his driveway winding down the hill. With a sigh of relief she turned up it.

There was a fire in the house. A fire burning bright and warm against the violence of the weather.

She started trying to plod more quickly, desperate for that warmth. Once again, she plummeted downward into the snow. Sputtering, she staggered back up. She touched her cheeks with her gloved fingers.

She couldn't feel them. . . .

She started forward again, so covered in the white flakes that she thought she must look like a giant snowman.

And then, still dreamily far away, she saw a door opening. A garage door, she realized dimly.

And the man was coming out.

He was carrying something.

She squinted against the snowflakes that fell against her face. What he carried was long, dark . . .

A shotgun?

And he was staring at her. Even from her distance she was sure she could feel the cutting blades of his eyes. And the violence and the fury about him seemed to reach out and touch her.

She paused, terrified, certain that this man did indeed intend harm to her.

She didn't care if she froze anymore. She only knew that she needed to escape.

She turned and started to run.

Running that hard should have hurt. But she couldn't feel her feet, just the shattering force against her knees as she pounded hard. The snow rushed all around her. She couldn't see anymore, and so she ran blindly. Her lungs seemed to be bursting, her forced breath changing to fog in the frosty air. There was a rush in her ears, a pounding, horrible, loud.

She lost the driveway. At some point she must have turned off it. She couldn't find the road, either, just aeons and aeons of white. She was plowing through the snow. It was up to her knees, then it was up to her waist.

The pounding continued. It was her heartbeat, she realized. She heard a rasp, but it wasn't the wind, it was the sound of her breathing.

"Stupid, idiot!" she heard suddenly.

Oddly enough, the snow was suddenly blackening before her. She was going to pass out, she thought.

"Idiot woman, stop!"

She didn't stop; she was too panicked. But even as she plunged forward, she realized that she must have been a glaring target in the snow in her jeans and red parka. If he had wanted to shoot her...

The logic couldn't really touch her. She saw a glare, and then blackness. A glare again...slowly fading. The blackness was closing in on her.

She ran on through the snow. Her foot caught on something, and then she was plunging into the snow. Deep, deep into the endless, icy, horrible cold. Into the shattering white... and into the endless blackness.

Dimly, she felt movement. She felt arms coming around her. She tried to blink. Her eyelids were so heavy. As if they were ice. Caked together.

She managed to open them.

She saw his eyes again. Deep, dark blue eyes. So dark they might have been obsidian, except that no one had eyes that dark. No, they were blue, and piercing, and condemning....

He was holding her in his arms. He was carrying her.

"No!" she managed to croak.

"I should have left you there!" he swore violently.

"I'll leave, I promise!"

"And how are you going to leave now? Honest to God, I should let you freeze! You were warned!"

"No, no, you don't—"

"I told you not to come!"

She shook her head, trying to remain conscious, trying to understand him, trying to make him understand her.

"Look, I don't know you!" she whispered. "I don't know what you're talking about. I don't—"

"Oh, shut the hell up, will you?"

The cap had moved back on his forehead. She could see his brows. They were high-arched, and ebony dark. And the scarf had slipped from his mouth. His jaw was square and firm, his cheeks lean and clean-shaven and strongly defined. His mouth was broad and generous; his teeth flashed white against his lips as he spoke.

But when he wasn't speaking...that mouth clamped down hard and firm, taut, grim, forbidding still. Terrifying. He was young. Not so young. Closer to forty than thirty.

His eyes were on the path ahead of him. He carried her as easily as he might a bag of groceries, and he seemed to be giving her no attention. Then his eyes were suddenly on her again, cutting her to the heart, slicing into her like ice.

"Why the hell did you run?"

Her teeth were chattering furiously. She didn't think she could answer him. "You—you were going to shoot me!"

"What?" he said incredulously.

"You were going to shoot me."

"With what?"

"I saw you with a gun—"

"You saw me with a shovel!"

Then he was swearing again, telling her what a fool she was, and that she deserved pneumonia or whatever else she might receive from her outing. "And so help me, God, lady, I swear you won't get a damned thing from me!"

"I don't want anything from you!" she cried.

"Keep up the lies and I will dump you right back into the snow!"

"Oh, will you listen to me, please? I swear I don't know what you're talking about! I don't know who's guilty of what, but I'm innocent, I swear..." Kristin began. But then it seemed that the snow filled her throat, and she couldn't speak again.

Her eyes were closing. She couldn't fight the snow anymore. She couldn't fight him.

And she couldn't fight the blackness anymore. It was a beautiful blackness. She was so cold, so horribly cold, but the blackness was still like a blanket of ice, wrapping around her, sheltering her, comforting her. It was easy to slip into it. Easy to welcome it. Easy to let the cold and the black take her away.

It was just so blissful not to fight anymore.

Her lashes lay still. Her eyes did not reopen.

Justin reached the front door and tore it open. It blew out of his hands and nearly off its hinges. He looked up. The sky was dark. Deadly dark. And the wind was keening now. Raging like a woman, crying like a banshee.

It had to be a nor'wester, careering out of Canada, sweeping them all by surprise. It was one of the most vicious storms he had seen in years.

He managed to step inside and slam the door behind him. He stood in the hallway for a moment, stamping his feet, trying to shake some of the snow from himself and from the woman in his arms.

He looked down at her face. It was white, almost as white as the snow. Little particles of ice seemed to have formed over the long heavy crescents of her sweeping lashes.

"Little idiot," he muttered. "I can't believe what you people are willing to go through to get a story! I told you not to come, and yet here you are risking your fool life!"

But she couldn't hear him, he realized.

Fool. He wanted to kill her, to throttle her, to shake some fury and some sense into her.

She was out cold, and her body was nearly frozen. Her pulse was weak. He shook his head again in disgust, amazed that any reporter would risk so much for a story. Then it occurred to him that she might be suffering from frostbite.

He had to warm her up.

Then he could kill her.

He carried her quickly into the huge porch that fronted the kitchen, laying her on the window seat. He discarded his hampering gloves and parka and set about removing her sodden red down jacket. He stared at her face again, and paused despite himself.

She looked like some ridiculous fairy princess. She was ashen with the cold, but he didn't think he'd ever seen more beautiful skin, fair and clear. Her mouth was well shaped, fully defined. Her lips were white now, too, but he was willing to bet that they would usually be a natural rosy red.

She was wearing no makeup. She didn't need any. Her lashes were so long and thick that they should have been illegal. And the whole of her face was a classic shape, something between a heart and an oval, wonderfully chiseled and clean and heart-stopping.

He tightened his jaw in a sudden new fury, wondering just what the hell else she might have been willing to use to deal with him for a story.

Idiot! According to most of the world, he was a murderer. What was the matter with her?

He let out a single expletive, then told himself to get on with warming her up. He really would have liked to leave her in the snow, but he couldn't. Because despite the opinion of the world, he wasn't a murderer.

She was soaked to the bone. She must have fallen in the snow a number of times. In front of the blazing fire, he stripped off her boots, her soaking socks, her jeans and her sweater.

She wasn't wearing a bra.

Her shoulders and breasts echoed the perfection of her face. Her throat was long and lean, her collarbones elegant, her shoulders fine and her breasts neither heavy nor small, but firm and shapely and crested by wide dusky-rose nipples that were hardened with the cold. Her torso was lean, ribs sweetly curving to a very small waistline, her hips flaring beneath it. Not too much. Just right. Sensually. Sexily. And beneath the lace bikini panties she wore he could just see a hint of a soft triangle of hair as dark and sable sleek as the mane upon her head.

He swore at her again, wondering why her beauty and perfection should so enrage him. Then he wrapped her in the afghan that lay by the window and cradled her in his arms to bring her as close to the fire as he could. Was she warm enough? he wondered. He chafed her feet, hoping against frostbite. Even her feet were exquisite. Not small, but slim, with neatly manicured toenails.

She was still cold. Her feet were not warming at all.

He carried her through the kitchen and dining room to the formal entry and then up the stairs to his huge bedroom suite. He passed through the sitting room to the bathroom. Still holding her, he turned on the water in the tub, making it hot enough to bring warmth quickly to her limbs, but not so hot that it would scorch her flesh.

The water rose quickly, and he slipped her into it, careful to rest her shoulders and head upon the rim. It was a whirlpool big enough for two, but despite the fact that he was wet and cold himself, he didn't think of joining her. He was growing worried that she might die on him. There was no way in hell to reach a hospital or a doctor—he couldn't even call for help. His electricity was holding out so far, but the phone had gone almost as soon as the storm started.

Yet even as he sat by her side, watching that her shoulders didn't slip, he began to see the color slowly creep back into her face. Her cheeks took on a soft blush. A natural rose came to her lips. He reached into the water and touched her foot, and found that it was warm. And her hands were warm and supple, too. Her nose was a little red with a windburn, but that was all, he was sure. She didn't awaken in the water, but she seemed more comfortable. He touched her wrist and found that her pulse was much stronger than it had been. And the color coming back to her was definitely a good sign.

He let out a shaky sigh of relief. No frostbite, no hypothermia. He touched her neck, and found that her pulse was now both regular and strong.

He released her, and looked at her with renewed anger. "Innocent, my ass!" he said. "Well, Miss Innocence, you were so damned determined on this course. Let's play it out. We'll even do it your way. It will be interesting to see just what course you intend to follow now that you've made it into the house. You want to play dangerously. Okay, sweetie. Let's play."

She moved slightly, a frown flitting over her beautiful brow. Then she was still again.

He grabbed a towel and lifted her from the water, wrapped her in the towel. He carried her out to his bed, stripping away the comforter and sheet. He dried her, trying not to be aware of the feel of her bare breasts against his arms.

Innocent.

She was built like pure temptation, like every sin in hell....

With the angelic beauty of her face.

Well, he had learned the hard way just what angelic beauty could hide.

He laid her back, hardened his jaw and decided to strip away the bikini panties. Why leave her in that little wisp of lace? Wet lace.

He eased the garment from her body. He meant to cover her instantly, but he didn't. He stepped back. Her legs were long and wickedly shapely, her lashes swept her cheeks....

Her breasts ... her hips ... the flare of alluring darkness at the juncture of her thighs ...

Her face, her lips ...

Her breasts, her thighs ...

He shook the comforter viciously and sent it flying over her.

It covered her face.

Leave it that way, he told himself.

No ... she could smother.

He smiled slowly, with a certain grimness, and a certain challenge. They were playing it her way. And it could be damned intriguing.

He had been accused of murder once already, he thought bitterly. That was why she was here. He certainly didn't want to make the charge viable by smothering one nosy little reporter.

He pulled the comforter from her face and tucked it warmly around her.

The heat was on, and still functioning. He had laid a fire for that night earlier. Now he went ahead and lit it, thinking that it might help.

He walked back to the bed and stared down at her. Again the purity of her beauty struck him, and he found himself gently smoothing the still damp tendrils from her brow. He wondered how long she would remain unconscious. She seemed to be in a natural sleep now, breathing easily. And her pulse remained steady and strong.

He turned away. He needed a hot shower himself. Then maybe he'd try to awaken her with a sip of brandy.

She wanted to play. . . .

Well, then, he thought, let the game begin.

And yet, even as he stripped off his sodden clothing and stepped beneath the warmth of the shower that fronted the huge tub across the marble floor, he felt a trembling within him, and a hot, hard, nearly blinding flash of desire.

It might well be a damned dangerous game for all involved.

Damned dangerous.

Chapter 2

Kristin was so comfortable. Warm, comfortable. The bed she lay upon supported her firmly, but cradled her body in softness. It was nice, so, so nice. The sheets were smoothly clean and smelled like the spring, and the blanket was wonderfully warm. She was deep, deep in the dark recesses of a lazy, sleepy comfort, and she did not want to leave it behind.

But she was awakening.

She opened her eyes, just barely. The world before her was still black. She realized that the sleek sheets she lay upon were black silk.

She didn't own any black silk sheets.

Neither did Roger and Sue.

The day came rushing back to her in a sweep of awful memory.

The flurries.

The blizzard.

The man. Oh God, the man!

And now she was stretched out on black silk sheets.

Where the hell was she?

Her eyes widened, her fingers tensed on the pillow. Beyond the bed a Persian carpet in creams and mauves lay on a hardwood floor. Farther away she could see a handsome fireplace with a fire blazing brightly. It was a contemporary room, uncluttered, handsome in its combinations of warm wood, black and cream.

A feeling of panic slowly began to overwhelm her. She didn't know where she was. She stared at her fingers and they suddenly seemed very pale and very small against the black silk of the pillowcase. Pale, and vulnerable, and naked...

Naked.

She realized that she could feel the silk against her flesh, all of her flesh.

She was naked. In some strange bed.

No, oh, no, oh, no...

It wasn't just a strange bed!

It was the maniac's bed!

She jerked up, numbed, frightened, her teeth suddenly chattering despite the warmth. And then she gasped in astonishment and screamed.

She wasn't alone.

He was in the room with her!

He, the maniac...

He was in the room with her, and she was stark naked on black sheets. He had been watching her sleep, watching her from the time her eyes began to open.

"It's all right, Miss—" he began.

She screamed again. Grabbing the covers to her chest, she scooted back on the bed as far away from him as she could go without rising.

"Hey!" he began again.

"Don't!" she cried, shimmying back even farther, her eyes wide with startled alarm. She tried to think coherently, but the only thing registering with her was a sense of sheer panic.

"Oh, come on!" he snapped impatiently. "Would you please stop that? I'm not even near you!"

Kristin realized then that he hadn't moved, that he hadn't really done anything that could be perceived as menacing.

He was just sitting there. Apparently he had been reading while waiting for her to awaken. He was across the room from the bed, about ten feet from the fire, sitting in a black crushed leather chair. He was wearing black jeans and a soft flannel plaid shirt, like a logger. And for the first time, she was seeing him without ten tons of winter paraphernalia about him.

He was still threatening though, she decided. He might not be making a single move, but he was very masculine-looking. Woodsy.

Kind of like the big bad wolf.

Her imagination was running wild, Kristin thought, determined to calm down.

But it was very hard to do so when she was naked between black silk sheets and staring at a stranger.

She tried to assess him rationally.

He wasn't as heavy as she had thought him. He was big, but built far more gracefully than she had imagined. His chest and shoulders were pleasantly broad, but he was leaner than he had previously seemed. And he didn't look wild or maniacal in any way. His black hair was neatly combed back from his face, and his features were strong but finely cut, lean and angular—with a broad mouth, full lips, wide-set shrewd eyes and a long straight nose.

He was really exceptionally good-looking, she thought with surprise. And as he stared at her and started to smile, she realized, too, that his smile was not without a certain charm.

"You really are all right," he said.

"I'm all right?" she repeated.

"Yes."

"I'm not all right!" she cried. "I'm confused, I'm miserable, I'm wretched, I'm . . . naked!"

His lashes swept down over his eyes, and she realized he was laughing at her. When he looked at her again, he was smiling. "Yes, that's true. I'm sorry—"

"Sorry!"

Oh, he ought to be smiling, all right! Kristin decided with sudden fury. He was like a cat playing with a mouse.

"If you just—" he began.

"What the hell is going on here?" she demanded heatedly.

His eyes darkened and narrowed. She reminded herself that even good-looking men could be maniacs, and this one still didn't seem to be entirely sane.

Except that if . . . if he had really intended to kill her or offer her definite harm, he could have done so already.

Of course, she didn't know exactly what had happened!

He dropped his newspaper and leaned forward, his hands folded tautly as he stared into her eyes.

"What the hell is going on here?" he repeated. "I should be asking you that. You came to my house, remember?"

"I didn't come to this room!"

"Well, I was trying to explain things to you, but maybe you're the one who ought to tell me, Miss . . ."

"Tell you what?"

"Your name, for starters."

"You don't know it?" she demanded.

"If I knew it, I wouldn't be asking."

"Well, you act as if you know everything else!" she accused him.

His fine hard jaw twisted at an angle. His blue eyes never left hers.

"I don't know your name. What is it?"

It couldn't hurt to answer that question, she decided, thinking quickly. She had to be careful. He was beginning to appear almost normal. And very attractive. She was still naked between his sheets, and very attractive and sensual men could still be maniacs. Just because this one was being a little more polite did not erase his previous behavior. And he was still looking at her with eyes cold and sharp enough to kill.

It was snowing outside. And she was naked in his house. It suddenly seemed best to answer him.

"Kristin. Kristin Kennedy," she told him. When he moved, she started again. He looked at her, surprised, grinning slowly. She cleared her throat. "And if you don't tell me what happened—"

"You know exactly what happened! You pretended that your car stalled out—"

"I didn't pretend anything!" she cried indignantly. A hot flush stained her cheeks. "And that's not what I'm talking about anyway. I mean—" Her voice broke off and she moved her hand over the black silk sheets. She felt her face growing to a fiery crimson.

Oh, Lord! If there were just anywhere to run! But there wasn't anywhere, there was a blizzard going on, and that was why she was here to begin with.

"Ah!" he said softly, watching as the color grew on her cheeks. "Let's go back. Kristin, is it?"

"Yes, it's Kristin! Except that it should be Ms. Kennedy to you."

"But we're very informal here, aren't we?" he asked pleasantly.

She wanted to scream. Her eyes narrowed and he laughed. "Relax, Ms. Kristin Kennedy. We were never that informal."

Relax. He was seriously telling her to relax. But the situation was still painfully informal to her. What was she doing in his bed—if it was his bed—and why was she in it the way she was?

"Then . . ." she began. She wanted to go further. The right words just wouldn't form on her tongue.

"You passed out on me," he told her. "I was afraid you were in for a serious case of frostbite or even lethal hypothermia. I took off your wet things and doused you in hot water."

"You . . . what?"

"Don't sound so damned indignant."

"Indignant! I'm furious! You had no right—"

"You had no right being here," he reminded her. "I was trying to save your life. And you weren't one bit of help. You're not exactly a lightweight," he added, and that last seemed to heap insult on top of injury.

"Oh! So I'm not exactly a lightweight! That's all that you have to say after—"

"I didn't mean that offensively. You're damned near perfectly built."

"Oh!" Kristin groaned. "You don't begin to grasp the seriousness—"

"I grasp it, you don't. You might have died, Ms. Kennedy!"

She might have. She fell silent, then pulled the covers more tightly about her.

"How long have I been ... sleeping?"

He glanced at his watch. "Umm, I think it was about noon when you began running away from me and my snow shovel. And it's past four now, so it's been several hours."

Hours. At least she hadn't lost days. It almost seemed as if she had, though.

She was accustomed to being on her own, to making her way through difficult situations. But she had never encountered a situation like this. Not with a man like this one.

He didn't seem to be offering her any harm at the moment. He probably had saved her life.

She was in an absolutely miserable position, and he knew it. And he wasn't making any attempt to make it easier for her. But then, he thought he had been extremely magnanimous in bringing her in from the cold.

He had done all that was necessary, just by saving her life.

What in God's name was it in his life that made him behave so strangely? Made him come after her so threateningly and furiously before?

Curiosity began to quell somewhat her fear. She was still wary. Very wary. But she seemed to be in one piece for the moment, and he was being almost polite.

He laughed again suddenly, and she thought that he really could be charming when he chose. His smile lit up his face, and brought a fascinating glimmer to his eyes. Something haunting ... sexy.

Umm. He was a very sexy man.

And she was even more distressed than she had been before.

"Four hours here, in this bed, alone...with you," she murmured.

"Yes—"

"Oh, no!"

"Not here with me in this bed. I mean I've been here with you. And you've been in this bed. Oh, never mind. I'm not going to be able to say the right thing no matter what," he told her. "Sorry, I really was trying to save your life. And don't keep staring at me like that. Beyond a doubt I wanted to throttle you, but beyond that, I like my women awake and very aware and involved—passionately involved. So you've got no worries on any of those little fantasies flashing through your mind."

"I don't have any fears or fantasies—"

"You're a liar," he told her bluntly. "But then, that's why you're here in all sorts of trouble wondering exactly what happened to you in my bed, right?"

"Stop it!" she cried out in frustration—and the very fear that she was denying. The slinky silk sheet started to slip. She snatched it back to her breasts quickly, staring at him with eyes that could have killed. "I am not a liar, and I'm telling you, I do not know what you're talking about."

"Right," he said agreeably. "You're not a reporter."

A vast uneasiness swept through her. She was a reporter. But how could he know that? And he seemed to think that he had talked to her before they met, and he had never, never talked to her before. She would certainly have remembered if he had.

But it was clear that she couldn't admit to being a reporter. She might find herself back in the snow.

"I swear to you, I do not know what you're talking about." There, she hadn't lied.

"I never told you not to come here?"

"I would have never asked you if I could come here!" she snapped. "I don't need your permission to travel on public roads. I was on my way to see my cousin, that's all. Can you comprehend that?"

"Right," he said.

He stood up. Instinctively, she backed away farther on the bed. He stopped, and the look he gave her suddenly shamed her. She had no reason to believe him, or believe in him, but she did. He had told her that he had merely warmed her, and she knew it was true. She didn't know why she was so convinced—the evidence that he was a maniac still seemed to be overwhelming. But he wasn't going to hurt her; she knew it. A soft flush covered her cheeks again.

"Sorry!" she said softly.

"Are you really so afraid of me?" he asked her, and it was with a curious tone. Almost a wary tone.

She shook her head. "No. I—I'm not. But I should be."

She almost jumped again when he placed his knee suddenly on the bed. He leaned dangerously close to her. His eyes were alive, sparkling like gems. And his smile was devilish, while tension seemed to leap from him like static.

"Why should you be?"

"Because you've threatened me enough!" she blurted quickly.

"That's right. You thought my shovel was a shotgun, right?"

"Well, I was plodding through the snow—"

"But I told you to drive away."

"Oh, you idiot! I tried to drive away!" She was ready to scream with frustration again. "I don't know who you think was coming here for what, but it wouldn't be worth it! Nothing would be worth this!''

"Not even one of the hottest scoops of the decade?" he suggested politely.

"Not even an exclusive interview with the Almighty!" Kristin assured him sweetly.

Was it the truth? Despite herself—and him—she was growing intrigued.

He arched a brow, but his tension had somewhat eased and he was smiling again. That handsome smile. Slow, sensual, dangerous. She realized that he had a pleasant scent about him, too. Nothing heavy or distinctive like an after-shave. He just smelled clean, as if he had recently showered. He had. His hair was still damp, she saw, and that was why the black locks were still staying back so neatly.

"Well, that's too bad," he said very softly. And his voice was husky, very husky. The sound of it sent curiously warm shivers streaking up and down her spine. "Because it seems that you're going to be stuck here for a while."

He straightened, walking to the cream-colored drapes that covered the windows. He pulled them back.

It was still snowing. Hard. The sky was dark gray, mixed with the white color of the snow that fell and fell and fell.

There must be endless inches of it upon the ground.

"Yes, you are certainly stuck here for a while," he said flatly.

She was stuck here. She felt her teeth start to chatter but then when she looked at him again, she realized she wasn't as frightened as she should have been.

In fact, she was growing far more fascinated with him than seemed right at all. Stay wary! she warned herself.

He was definitely still wary of her. He hadn't begun to believe a word that she was saying.

"May I borrow your phone?" she asked him.

He shrugged. "You're welcome to borrow it," he told her. "But it won't do you a bit of good. It hasn't worked since this storm first whipped up."

"Oh," she breathed. She glanced at the glowing lamp. He smiled again, this time with a slightly mocking curve, as if he sensed that she doubted his word.

"I imagine the electricity will go soon enough," he told her.

He walked around the bed, picking up the receiver of a cream phone that sat on the nightstand by the bed. He handed it to her. She placed it against her ear, and heard nothing but dead silence. She stared at him, and he laughed.

"I didn't fix the phone or pull the plug or the like, Ms. Kennedy. I'm trying to get rid of you, not keep you in prison here," he reminded her lightly.

"I didn't call you a liar," she said sweetly. "You're the one who keeps calling *me* a liar."

"I'm not a liar, just a dangerous lecher, right?" he asked.

"You're just incredibly rude," she replied flatly.

He laughed again, and the sound was easy and pleasant. "Well, excuse me, Ms. Kennedy!"

"Oh, I am trying very hard to do just that!"

"It is my house," he reminded her.

"So it is. And since you keep accusing me of the stupidity of driving through a snowstorm just to reach you, why don't you tell me why you imagine anyone would want to do so?"

"I'm still not convinced that you didn't do just that," he said, but his tone remained pleasant.

"I think you're an egomaniac!" she announced.

"Ah, well, that's better than a madman."

"Ah, but I think that term might just fit you as well," Kristin blurted.

"Yes, indeed. One of those madmen who shoot with their shovels, right?"

She flushed and shrugged. There seemed little reason to deny it.

He changed the subject. "Was this cousin of yours expecting you?" he asked suddenly.

"Yes, eventually," Kristin said. "I didn't tell him exactly when I was coming. I'm not late enough for him to call out the National Guard, or anything."

"Good," he said very softly.

Why had she just admitted that? She should have said that Roger would soon be combing the woods for her!

"One would hate to think of a relative risking this storm to rescue you!" he said dryly.

He was standing near her back. She spun around, suddenly feeling a series of little hot sizzles against her naked back. He obviously didn't believe a word of what she had told him.

But he was still smiling. And he was still completely charming with his deep blue gaze and slow curling lip.

"Want something to eat?" he asked her suddenly.

"Pardon?"

"I said, are you hungry? Do you want something to eat?"

She realized that she was ravenous. "Wow, you mean you'd actually feed me?" she asked with a wide-eyed innocence. "You've already let me in the house. Are you sure that you want to offer that much hospitality."

"I've already let you into my house, my bathtub and my bed," he corrected her, grinning as his comment sent new color to suffuse her cheeks. "Still suspicious!" he said, arching a knavish brow. "But then that's good, isn't it? It probably wouldn't pay for either of us to be off our guard now, would it?"

Kristin was suddenly determined to gain some dignity around this man. "I'm telling you, sir, I really do not know what you're talking about. And you probably did save my life, and I'm extremely grateful that you did so. Whatever it took. I like living."

"My, my," he murmured softly. "That sounded like a thank-you. From a reporter. What a surprise."

"Reporters are people," Kristin said stiffly.

"Not in my book." The comment was as hard and certain as steel.

"It sounds as if you've been maligned by scandal sheets—" Kristin began.

"A reporter is a reporter, Ms. Kennedy. I don't care who sent you here—"

"No one sent me here!" she wailed in exasperation.

"Well, then, Ms. Kennedy, yes, since you are here, I do want to offer you the hospitality of a meal. I'm starving, myself. And as rude as I may be, I don't want to eat in front of you. And the electricity most probably will fail very soon, so I think I'll go down and get started on something. Feel free to join me anytime."

He started to leave the room. He was going to leave her. Alive and well and unmolested.

Kristin caught her covers more tightly to her chest and moved forward, calling after him. "Wait! Please, where are my things? I, er, I can't come down like this."

His eyes moved over her quickly, then met hers again. It wasn't a licentious stare in any way, but she still had a feeling that he remembered her very well.

"There are some robes in the closet. Pick out whatever you like. Your clothes are still sopping wet. I didn't think to put them in the dryer, but I'll do that now, too."

He started to leave the room again, then hesitated, pointing to a door. "The bath is there. There's a door out to the hallway through a dressing room from the bath, or you can come through the sitting room, this way. There's a cabinet beneath the sink in the bath where I'm pretty sure there are new toothbrushes and toothpaste and the like. Make yourself at home."

"Thank you," Kristin told him, amazed. He seemed such a far cry from the man who had told her that she was welcome to freeze out in the snow because it would be her own fault if she did so. "Thank you, really, Mr. — " She broke off. She didn't know his name.

"I'm sorry," she murmured. "I never even asked you your name."

"You didn't?" He arched a brow, and smiled. There seemed something wary about that smile again. "It's Magnasun. Justin Magnasun."

"Thank you, Mr. Magnasun."

He was staring at her. Pointedly. As if she had known what his name was all along. As if he were waiting for her to make some comment upon it.

But the name Justin Magnasun didn't mean a thing to her.

"Justin," he told her pleasantly. "After all, we are in close quarters."

"Justin," she said, her teeth grating. He was looking at her like the cat who had wolfed down the canary, trying for a rise out of her. He wasn't going to get it.

"Thank you, Justin," she said. She smiled sweetly, innocently.

He arched a brow. "My name doesn't mean anything to you?" he asked.

"Not a thing. Should it?"

"It's known in certain circles."

"Sorry. I must not be in those circles." She smiled again. "Would you like me to cook dinner for you? I'm a good cook."

"You don't mind cooking for me?"

"You didn't mind—er—saving my life."

"Oh, I didn't mind in the least," he assured her. He grinned, the devil's own grin. "It seems we've come a long, long way already, Kristin," he said, and left the room at last, closing the door behind him.

Kristin stared after him, exhaled slowly and then leaped to her feet. She hurried across the room to the closet he had indicated and threw open the door.

The closet was a huge walk-in room with racks on either side, rows of shoes on the floor and shelving for sweaters and knits on the top. It was pleasantly scented with cedar.

She discovered herself running her fingers over the tweed fabric of a jacket while she searched through the hangers for a robe. She found one, white terry cloth, and pulled it down. It probably came just past his knees. It would cover her nearly to her ankles. She slipped it around her body as quickly as she could, hugging it to her.

This was strange. So very, very strange.

She started to shiver, wondering if her ordeal in the cold hadn't affected her mind. Justin Magnasun was frightening. He suspected her of being a reporter who had braved severe hazards to get to him.

The irony was that she was a reporter. Not the reporter he was expecting, but...

She remembered the tone of his voice when he had stated that no reporter—no matter what kind—was quite human, in his book.

She had best never, never admit to him that she was one of their number.

Dummy! she thought in silence. He really didn't know reporters at all! She was a good one, and she was proud of herself, and she was very proud of the number of things that she had done. Her series of investigative articles had brought attention to the plight of the aged in certain nursing homes. She had brought a whole town around to donate the money for a child's operation. She'd done good and meaningful work, and this man was maligning not just her, but her colleagues—most of whom were diligent, hardworking and caring individuals!

He had thought she should recognize his name.

Why?

She closed her eyes tightly and tried to remember. No, the name meant nothing to her. Nothing at all.

She sighed, determined that she had to be very careful around him, no matter how charming his smile could be. She touched her cheeks and found they were warm and flushed again. He'd stripped her clothing from her and put her to bed. He was nonchalant about it, but he'd commented that he thought that she was perfect. . . .

"Stop!" she whispered out loud to herself.

She belted the robe securely about her and hurried out of the closet. She saw the door that he had indicated led to the bathroom and she strode quickly across to it. When she had thrown open the door, she paused again.

It was an extraordinary bath. Like the bedroom, it was done in shades of black and cream with small red accents. Against the far wall was a huge whirlpool tub. The spigots were brass, and the steps leading up to it were sleek black tile. The tile on the flat part of the floor was white. There was a shower stall in a smoked-glass and brass enclosure, and the commode was enclosed as well. The double sinks were in a center island under a skylight. All the skylight offered now was a vision of gray, but the effect of the room was still overwhelming. Mr. Magnasun had to be a man of means to afford such handsome opulence.

She gave herself a mental shake and delved into the cabinet beneath the sink for a toothbrush and toothpaste. She stared at her reflection in the mirror as she studiously brushed her teeth, but finally her hand stopped moving and she just stared.

Who was he? she wondered. Curiosity was burning like a fire within her. He was rich and striking, with a temper like wildfire, and the capability of being as smooth as Cary Grant.

He was certain she was a reporter after a story.

Which meant there was a story to be had.

He didn't want his story told, whatever it was.

But she had to know....

No. She didn't have to know.

She had to be careful until the snow stopped, until she could get away.

She rinsed out her mouth, found soap and a washcloth and bathed her face. She hadn't come to get anything from him.

She had gotten into trouble here, and it seemed he had helped her despite his suspicions. She couldn't go delving into his life.

She was going to have to delve into his life.

No.

Yes.

With a sigh she dug back beneath the sink, looking for a brush. There wasn't one there. She walked back into his bedroom and found one on his black walnut dresser. Before the fire, she started to brush out her hair, and then she stopped.

She was comfortable here. Comfortable in a strange man's bedroom, with the fire blazing so warmly. Comfortable in his bath, because it was such a beautiful place with such sleek lines. She had been so comfortable that she had just picked up his brush to use.

She put it back down on his dresser quickly, and moved her hand away as if the brush had suddenly come to life.

She didn't want to think about how easy it was to feel that she was on informal terms with this stranger.

Kristin pulled the belt more tightly on the robe and hurried out of the bedroom. As he had told her, she walked into a sitting room. And there she paused again and frankly stared at the fireplace and the black walnut desk, at the rows and rows of bookshelves and the two deep black leather armchairs set against rich cream rugs. There was a stereo system and a large-screen television that could be seen from the chairs, or if someone was stretched out on the deep plush rugs. She could almost imagine a fire blazing and two people curled together, enjoying music or a movie or just watching the fire crackling.

She'd better watch it. She was falling in love with a house. A house she needed to leave as quickly as possible.

She opened the sitting room door to discover herself in an open hall with a curved staircase that led downward to the first floor. She could see the entry to the house from where she stood, for the open hallway looked out over the door and the dusky gray tiles there. She followed the stairs down to that entry, and from there down a few steps to the living room. She paused, staring once again.

Beyond the living room, large plate-glass windows showed a huge turquoise pool to the rear of the living room. It, too, was enclosed in glass. There was a patio surrounding it with comfortable deck chairs, there was a large barbecue, there was a whirlpool at one end of the pool, and water cascaded in an elegant fall from the whirlpool into the main body of crystal-clear water.

Against the darkness and the snow outside, the pool was beautiful. And against the pool, the darkness and the snow were equally fascinating.

"Do you like it?"

Kristin whirled around.

Justin Magnasun stood in a doorway at the far end of the living room, watching her with intense curiosity in his eyes.

"You've a really beautiful house."

"Thank you," he said almost curtly. "Come on through here. The kitchen is this way."

She followed him through the doorway to a kitchen that would have been anyone's dream, from the center island range and grill to the state-of-the-art conveniences, to the rows of copper cookware hanging from ceiling hooks.

Beyond the kitchen was a large sun room with a tile floor, completely encircled with window seats. The windows looked out to the front of the property. Without the snow, Kristin thought, the view would go on forever.

"This is wonderful!" she gasped. She spun around with enthusiasm. "So secluded, every comfort..."

She broke off because he was studying her again so intently.

"This is a great kitchen, state of the art," she told him flatly. "And it's all just for you."

He returned her stare without answering.

She realized she wasn't going to get any answers from him—not now—and ground down hard on her teeth. She wasn't supposed to ask questions. Well, she didn't care about his damned story. She hadn't come here for a scoop.

They stared at each other for a long hard moment. Then he turned away and asked casually, "Red wine or white, Ms. Kennedy?"

"I don't know. What am I cooking?"

His anger seemed quick to fade. Either that, or he baited her constantly. He flashed her a quick smile and extended a hand toward the refrigerator. "Your choice."

She walked past him and opened the refrigerator, which seemed fairly well supplied. And there was a spice rack on the wall, so she could get creative.

She smiled and looked at him. "Spiced beef with vegetables," she told him. "A nice burgundy would be good."

"Spiced beef with vegetables?" he inquired doubtfully.

She nodded.

"Well," he murmured softly, "if you can really make it taste as good as it sounds, saving you from the snow might turn out to be extremely worthwhile."

"It will taste better than it sounds," Kristin promised him.

He brushed past her, reaching for a bottle of wine that lay in a built-in rack. She felt his scent whisper softly over her again. Clean, masculine. Simple. And very alluring in that simplicity.

Food, she reminded herself. She didn't intend to become too intrigued with the man.

You're supposed to remain intelligently frightened and very wary! she reminded herself.

She wasn't intrigued, surely she wasn't. He had been far too rude initially. And he was still watching her constantly, convinced that she was someone else.

A reporter. Ouch. It was very dangerous here.

"Spiced beef..." she murmured. She delved into the refrigerator for all the ingredients she had seen that she could use. She began piling things on the counter. She turned and discovered that he was right behind her. He had poured the wine and was offering her a glass.

Her fingers curled around it, brushing his. He smiled, standing so close to her that they nearly touched. She felt warmth emanating from him.

"Cheers, Ms. Kennedy," he said. He sipped his wine, and urged her glass to her lips. She swallowed the wine and it, too, was warm. Very warm. It seemed to bring heat racing throughout her. A heat that flashed between them, that seemed to tempt her to come nearer and nearer.

He stepped away from her suddenly, as if he had felt it, too.

As if it had been far too tempting. And as his eyes remained on hers, she remembered that he had her at an advantage.

He had seen far more of her than she had of him.

He had even called her perfect....

"I'll leave you to this culinary masterpiece of yours, Ms. Kennedy. I'll be anxiously awaiting its completion in the den. Call me if you need me."

He turned and left her then.

But the warmth of his nearness seemed to linger on the air.

And dance along her spine...

And settle somewhere within her. Somewhere deep, deep within her.

Who are you? she wanted to shout after him. And why are you so damned wary of reporters?

The question would get her nowhere then, she knew.

But the snow was still falling outside. Falling with a vengeance. She didn't need to be told that they were in the midst of a good blizzard. She had hours—maybe days—of discovery before her.

Days...

She trembled suddenly, and she wondered if it was because she was dreading the time ahead with him....

Or if she was anxious for it to come.

Chapter 3

Although she had feared that the electricity might fail her, it held while Kristin cooked their meal.

Since her unwilling host had disappeared, she felt free to roam through the cabinets at will. He didn't seem to be missing a thing. He had every gourmet convenience in the world, and even when she had found everything she needed for the simple meal she was making, she continued to probe cabinets. She just couldn't resist. Beyond the usual food processing equipment, he had a beautiful copper-scrolled cappuccino and espresso maker, special spice grinders, an ice cream maker, a pasta machine and any number of other wonderful kitchen gadgets.

She made her spiced beef in the wok and prepared some fried rice to go with it. She stared out the front windows of the beautiful sun porch as she worked. There wasn't even a hint of sun to be seen. Night had come with the weather. It was nearly black out, with the snow barely visible now in that darkness except where it slammed against the window.

Some flurries, she thought.

With her feast prepared, she began to wonder where he would want to eat it, and just what he might want to eat it on. He hadn't walked in on her once. But just as she was about to go in search of him, he appeared in the doorway again. It was uncanny. Almost as if he had been watching her.

But then, she reflected, maybe he really had been watching her. Maybe he had appeared while she was diving into all his cabinets. Maybe she simply hadn't seen him.

He could move so silently when he wanted to. It was unnerving.

He didn't seem angry, though. He was just watching her, with that endlessly speculative light to his eyes. Tall, broad, confident, he leaned against the doorway, and she knew then that he had been there for more than a little while.

And then he smiled. "Is dinner all done?"

"All done."

"Let's take our plates into the living room," he suggested. "There's a weather report coming up."

"Wonderful," she agreed. "What plates?"

"I could swear I've got dozens of plates in the cabinets," he told her.

"Yes," she said, flushing. He did have dozens of plates in the cabinets. "It's just that I don't know what plates you meant to use for something this casual. I mean, you may have good plates that you don't just use for every day."

He gazed at her with an amusement that actually bordered on the friendly. "If it's there, Ms. Kennedy, it's there to be used. I don't believe in having things just to have them.''

She felt her lips curling into a smile. There was just something about him. She didn't want to trust him. Not in the least. She didn't want to lose one bit of her wariness. His smile was just so damned charming. And his voice could carry such a deep and husky edge. If she'd only met him under other circumstances, she could have been swept right off her feet.

"That's nice," she murmured. "I don't believe in having things just to have them, either."

"Glad you approve," he replied. And then it seemed that they stood there, staring at each other.

He didn't trust her, and he didn't want to trust her. But she felt that even as he watched her, he seemed to feel something curious, too. An elusive draw to her despite everything...

Umm. Your basic lust. So elusive a draw, she taunted herself. But it was true. She found him very sensual—beguiling. There lay the danger.

And while he might not like her, or trust her...it seemed he felt a curious draw, too.

She suddenly felt very desperate to back away.

But then he spoke, breaking whatever it was that had come between them. "Okay, I'll tell you what. I'll get the plates."

He pulled down a pair of plates with a beautiful pattern and set them on the island. He breathed in the scent of the spiced beef that she had spooned from the heat of the wok to cool in a crockery bowl. He glanced at her again. "If it tastes as good as it smells, you really can cook," he told her.

She shrugged. "I try."

"What else do you try?"

"Pardon?" she asked, fighting for composure. She'd heard him. She'd heard him perfectly well. But the question had seemed to cast chill fingers right around her heart. She didn't dare answer him. He hated reporters with a passion. And he was surely baiting her, because she was certain that he hadn't believed a word of her real story.

And he still might be a maniac. A sensual, striking maniac, but a maniac.

He smiled at her response to his question. She couldn't begin to read the meaning of that smile. "What do you do, Ms. Kennedy? What do you do for a living?"

"Oh, I dabble in a few things. Actually, I'm between jobs," she murmured, then quickly changed the subject. "Hurry up and dish out a plate before it gets too cold."

He prepared himself a plate, then took hers and fixed it for her, too. "The wine is already out by the fireplace. Just grab our glasses."

In a few minutes they were settled before the fire, watching the news on a large-screen television. Kristin had found it most comfortable to sit cross-legged on the floor; Justin Magnasun was on the sofa behind her. The fire snapped and crackled warmly, and the wine was fine and dry and warming, too.

It would be easy to feel very comfortable and relaxed here, she thought.

But she mustn't. She didn't know him. And she didn't know a thing about him. She was very aware of him, sitting so close behind her that he could reach out and touch her. She could feel him there, despite the bit of distance between them. She felt nervous tremors again, hot and then cold. His hands were fascinating. Handsome, large bronzed hands with short, neatly clipped nails. She couldn't help wondering how they would feel against her naked flesh. And then her tremors would run very hot, and she would try not think about him at all. She gave her attention to her food and to watching the broadcast about the snow ravaging the city.

The same newsman who had so blithely mentioned the possibility of flurries was on the screen again.

The story had changed, of course. It was a blizzard, a full-scale blizzard. Cars were stuck all over New England. Rescue services were doing their best, but it was difficult with the storm in full force. Phone and power lines were down, and in the outlying regions of the state, it could be a good week before roads were cleared and utilities restored.

And according to the weatherman now, he had suspected that morning that the lighter snow in the forecast would become something far more serious.

"Why didn't he say so then?" Kristin blurted aloud.

"He says he did," Justin said lightly from behind her.

She swung around, her eyes sparkling, ready for battle. "He most certainly did not!"

The wine was giving her a fine new courage. She set her plate down and rose to her feet, hands on her hips, accosting him. "I'm telling you, Mr. Magnasun, I most certainly did not start out from Boston this morning planning to have car trouble right in front of your house! I'd have to be a complete fool to do something like that. What if my car had died a mile earlier, a mile later? I would have risked my life!"

"Some people think a good story is worth risking a lot for," he responded, staring at her evenly.

"I happen to be fond of living," she informed him. She spun around then, picking up her plate and her wineglass and heading back to the kitchen, her hair flying out in a wild fluff behind her as she did so.

She gasped when she felt his hand on her arm, stopping her, spinning her around.

His eyes were like a blue blaze, his bronze features were tense. "You swear it?" he demanded suddenly.

She stared from his eyes to the fingers that wound so tightly around her flesh. Then she stared back into his eyes. The fire from them seemed to leap out and touch her. To sizzle through her flesh and blood and touch her soul.

"Do I swear what?" she demanded.

"That you didn't come here on purpose! That you're not that little scandal hound I spoke to on the phone!"

"I swear it!" she snapped. She was suddenly afraid for him to touch her. Not because he was hurting her. But because of that sizzling fire she felt between them.

She broke free and went on through the kitchen. She turned the water on high and squirted a liberal amount of dish detergent into the sink.

She was startled to feel him behind her. "I'll do the dishes, Ms. Kennedy."

"I'm fine."

"You're better than fine," he said lightly. "You're perfect. But you did the cooking. I'll clean up."

"Oh, but you saved my life, remember? Surely that's worth cooking and cleaning up in return."

"I definitely remember saving your life. I don't think I'll ever forget," he told her huskily.

She could feel his vibrant presence at her back. Feel the timbre of his voice, the heat of his body.

He backed away, still speaking. "Let's clean up together, then. There's a great movie coming on. A classic whodunit. It will be a nice way to pass an evening."

He wasn't waiting for her to agree. He left her with the soap-filled sink and found a sponge to clean out the wok. There wasn't much to do, and in a matter of minutes, the kitchen was cleaned up. Justin watched her fold up a dish towel.

"Want something hot?"

She arched a brow. "Something hot?" At times, there just didn't seem to be anything hotter than him.

"Coffee, tea, cappuccino?"

"If you do, I suppose," she murmured uneasily.

"Then go on out. I'll have it in a minute."

She looked at him blankly, then challenged him.

"So have you decided to believe me, then?"

He stared at her, seemed about to speak, then paused, a crooked smile curving his lip. "Not really."

"Then—" she began in a fury.

"Hold it! You tell me—do you believe in me?"

"I never accused you of anything!"

"Not with words. But I've seen it in your eyes. You've accused me of just about everything you can accuse a man of being or doing. Do you suddenly trust me? Completely?"

"No," she breathed after a moment, still meeting his gaze.

"Well, we've come to a certain honesty. Let's call it a truce, eh?"

He came to her and turned her around by the shoulders. She wanted to retain her anger and indignation with him. Both seemed to drain away far too quickly. She liked the feel of him. He smelled so good. And it was very nerve-racking having him touch her so.

"I didn't tell you thank-you, did I?" he whispered softly. The sound just touched her ears. The whisper of his breath was warm, and caused a stirring within her.

More than a stirring. That single whisper made her think of all sorts of things that she shouldn't be thinking about.

"Dinner was...delicious," he finally added. He made it sound as if dinner had been an entirely sensual affair.

He was baiting her, she thought. She needed to be even more careful.

Then he gave her a little prod, urging her from the kitchen. Kristin returned to the living room, pulling his robe more tightly about her. She curled up on the floor where she had been, to watch the television. The movie coming on was a great old Hitchcock. It was the perfect picture for watching before a fire on a snow-filled night.

A moment later Justin reappeared, carrying matching mugs with sticks of rock candy protruding from them. He sat down beside her, cross-legged on the floor, and handed her one.

"Cappuccino. I had it once with the rock candy and thought it was great."

Kristin sipped it. It was great cappuccino.

"Do you cook much?" she asked him.

"Not much. I make cappuccino and espresso, but that's mostly because the machine does the work."

Kristin took another sip. She was going to question him again, but she couldn't miss the opportunity. "That's a very elaborate setup you have."

"Yes, it is."

"Do you live with someone else?"

He smiled. "No, I live alone."

"But—"

His eyes were level on hers. "Why the curiosity, Ms. Kennedy? Are you writing a book?"

"No, Mr. Magnasun. If I were writing a book on you, I'd already have the answers to questions as simple as that one!"

He arched a brow. She realized how she must have sounded. "I forgot. It's a truce."

"Yes. We've agreed to be entirely unsuspicious of each other."

She smiled. He was damned suspicious.

He was also suddenly the perfect host. And the closer she came to him, the more she felt a compelling attraction. A lock of his ebony hair fell softly over his forehead. He had that wonderful clean scent about him, and he was striking and warm in his plaid shirt with his bright blue eyes.

She realized suddenly that she wanted to trust him. That she was attracted to him. Far more than she had been attracted to a man since...

Ever.

Careful...

And still, the time seemed to pass easily as she sat there listening to him, covered in his terry robe, sipping his wonderful cappuccino before the fire.

This was the same man who had ranted and raved to her out in the snow, she reminded herself. The maniac who had thrown her out of her car to get it started for her. The same man who had it in for a certain reporter, and who still seemed convinced that she was that reporter and that she had been willing to brave death to get a story from him.

What in God's name was that story?

If she valued life and limb and sanity, she'd best be careful that she didn't find out too much about him.

But she had to know....

Not tonight, she decided. According to the fool who had warned her about the "flurries," they were now in the midst of a full-scale blizzard.

She might be here for a long, long time.

"On the other hand," he was saying, watching her with a simple curiosity, "you're a really talented cook. That was an incredible meal to just whip up in minutes."

She grinned. "My grandfather was a pastry chef, and he really was talented. That's how he managed to get into this country."

"From Ireland?"

"The name is Kennedy," she agreed with a laugh.

"Any relation to *the* Kennedys?"

She shook her head. "Not that I know about. Grandda came over in 1929 with one of the big hotels as his sponsor. He worked until the day he died, and he loved to cook. I loved him, so I would sit in his kitchen whenever I could while I was growing up. Some of his knowledge simply rubbed off."

"Did you ever think about being a chef yourself?"

"No," Kristin began, but then she remembered she couldn't tell him what she really did for a living. "Well, I do some catering now and then," she told him. It was almost true. When her family got together, there was easily a party of fifty or more. And sometimes she did do the cooking.

"A jack-of-all-trades?" he asked. "Sorry, a jill-of-all-trades?"

"Not all of them. Maybe a few. Oh, the movie is starting!" she said with relief. He was watching her too intently.

She sipped her cappuccino. There was a delicate taste of almond to it.

He seemed to sense her question before she asked it. "Amaretto," he told her. "Just a touch. It seemed right before the fire, and neither of us is driving anywhere tonight."

No, she wouldn't be driving anywhere. But she still needed her wits about her. . . .

"It's good," she told him. He smiled. He always seemed to sense her thoughts. She looked quickly to the television screen.

The movie had come on, and they both started to watch it. They were quiet for a while, comfortably quiet. They were sitting side by side on the floor, using the sofa as a backrest. The fire blazed cheerfully, the movie was good, the cappuccino was warm and delicious and lulling. A sense of well-being settled over Kristin, and as she watched the suspects dramatically gather on the screen, she delicately licked at her stick of rock candy.

Then she sensed that Justin was watching her. She almost froze, and her eyes rose to his. The tip of her tongue was just touching a clear square of the candy. She froze for a minute.

And then she felt the touch of his gaze warm her. Slowly, completely. From head to toe . . . and in between. She felt a fluttering in her stomach that moved deeper and deeper as his eyes remained on her. He didn't really touch her, not at all, just with his eyes. . . .

And yet she'd never felt a more sensual touch upon her flesh.

Never.

She had ceased even to breathe, she realized, gasping in air at last.

Then he placed his fingers on hers. He took the stick of candy from her and set it back in her mug. And his hand cupped around her cheek.

He was going to kiss her. She knew it because of the way he looked at her, and she knew it because she had never felt anything so much like lightning as the tension that seemed to snap and sizzle on the air. She knew because she had never wanted anything in her life as much as she wanted him to touch her now, right now....

She should have opened her mouth and protested furiously. She should have jumped up and run. She should have stopped him. It was insane.

But she wanted it....

Wanted to feel his lips, the fire and sear of his kiss, the caress of his touch.

His lips formed over hers.

Suspicion, fear...

Desire...

They all warred within her.

The fascination that had been slowly building inside her allayed all other emotion. She was a fool. The words haunted her mind, but did not still her longing for his touch. She did not protest.

His fingers splayed across her cheek, his lips just touched down on hers. Touched down and parted them, and the tip of his tongue slipped between her lips, hot and wet, and just touched hers.

Teased... touched. Moved against her more fully, more deeply. Tasted, explored.

She arched to the touch. She savored the texture of his lips, of his tongue. Mesmerized, she felt his fingers move over her face. Felt them massage sensually into her hair. Felt his lips break from hers, touch them again.

And then she looked into his eyes. They were so very blue. Searching...

And fascinated. Whatever the draw that pulled her to him so innately, he felt it, too. And wondered at it.

She moistened her lips, for he continued to search out her eyes.

Sanity suddenly returned. She jumped to her feet. He watched her as she drew her hand to her mouth, as a stricken light appeared in her eyes.

"We can't be doing this!" she gasped.

"Why?"

"I don't even know you."

"And I don't know you," he agreed.

"You despise who you think I am!"

He was silent for a moment and she knew that it was true, he still didn't believe her, truce or no.

"How could you!" she breathed in sudden anger. "Someone you condemn so thoroughly! Someone you hate—"

"I don't hate you!" he snapped. Hands on his hips, he stared at her across the room.

"You don't believe in me!"

"But damn you!" he said in return, his voice soft, very, very soft. "I do want you!"

At least he was being honest when he said that. At least one thing was open between them. Maybe his words should have made her even angrier than she already was. But they didn't. Anger at them would have been hypocritical.

She shook her head slowly. "Well, don't want me, Mr. Magnasun. Don't—"

"You responded damned quickly!" he told her through clenched teeth.

"Yes, I did. But I won't again. I admit that you've got ... something. Still, it's just not that simple to me. Wanting means at the very least respecting someone. Enjoying them, laughing with them, trusting them—"

"It doesn't mean any of those things," he interrupted her quietly. "Maybe going with the emotion hinges on them, but wanting someone . . . well, that just happens."

It did just happen. She had wanted him. But she needed to believe that it was more. And maybe it was. She hated to admit it to herself, but she liked him. And as difficult as it should have been, she was discovering that it was very easy to want to trust him, to trust in him.

He swept out a hand suddenly. "Shall we see the rest of the movie? Have a seat. Over there. Far over there." He smiled. And as angry as she had been, she couldn't help but smile, too. Distance was good.

She sat across the room, against a chair. He tossed her a pillow, and leaned back himself, staring at the screen.

"Damn, this is difficult," he said after a while.

She didn't answer him. She watched the screen, and she listened to the snap and crackle of the fire.

"Justin," she said.

"What?"

"Why do you have that great kitchen all for yourself?"

He was quiet for only a minute. "Well, when I envisioned this place, I wanted it to have everything. I thought that it could be a real home one day. Where two people might have everything."

Curious, Kristin reflected on his words. "Were you— married? Or planning on being married?"

She could see him stiffen. So tautly that she was suddenly afraid again. "Look, I'm sorry if I—"

"Not now."

"What?"

"I'm not married now, nor planning on marriage," he said harshly.

"I didn't mean to offend you," she said at a loss.

Suddenly his eyes were on her. Sharp. Very blue. "What about you?"

"Pardon?"

"Are you married?"

"No," she murmured, flushed.

"Engaged? Living with a 'significant other'?"

Was he mocking her? Once again, he was watching her intently, looking for...something.

"No," she said softly.

"Good," he said. "At least..."

"At least what?"

"At least what happens will be between the two of us, no one else involved." He looked back to the screen before she had a chance to worry about his statement. "Let's watch this, shall we? They're gathering together again for the unmasking of the murderer."

"Ah, but I know the end," she said. "It's one of my favorite classics."

"Next to *Arsenic and Old Lace*," he said.

"And *Harvey!*"

To Kristin's amazement, they went on with their light war over classic movies. Then their comments came farther and farther apart. She closed her eyes, tired. More comfortable than she should have been.

Then her eyes suddenly flew open. She was trying to awaken as she felt herself being lifted.

He was carrying her again.

"Hey! It's all right," he said to her look of alarm. "You fell asleep. I'm just putting you to bed." He grinned. "Alone."

"Oh," she said awkwardly. "I can walk. You don't have to carry me up the stairs." No, he didn't have to carry her. It was so intimate. And too damned comfortable. She had to curl her arms around his neck. And she still liked the feel and the scent of him, and it would still be way too easy to . . .

"I don't mind."

"You told me before that I wasn't exactly a lightweight."

He grinned slowly. "Well, maybe I exaggerated just a little bit."

"Where are you taking me?"

"Back to my room." His grin deepened as her eyes widened. "Don't worry. I'll be in the guest quarters."

"I'll sleep there. I don't want to throw you out of your own room."

"You're not throwing me out."

"But I shouldn't take your room—"

"It doesn't matter."

"You wanted to leave me in the snow," she reminded him.

"That was then. This is now."

He carried her up the stairs and set her down in the doorway to the bedroom. "I'll be right down the hall if you need me." He stood close to her. Very close.

"Good night."

"Wait," she said.

He paused. "Yes?"

She hesitated, then her curiosity prodded her on. "Just what was this story about that I'm supposed to have risked all to delve into?"

He stood there, watching her. Then he turned and started walking away.

"Justin!"

He paused and called something softly over his shoulder. She couldn't hear what he said, but it had been an answer.

Kristin felt tension flash through her body.

"Wait!" she cried out. She raced after him, but he ignored her. He walked down the hall and opened another door. "Wait!" she cried again, still running after him. He paused in the doorway. "You actually answered me! But what did you say?"

He stared at her. "You swore you didn't come for a story."

"I didn't! But you said something—"

"I said murder."

"What!"

"I said that the story would be about a murder," he told her bluntly.

Amazement seared through her. Well, she had thought his behavior maniacal at first. But . . .

No, he couldn't have committed a murder. She didn't know him! But, yes, she did, in a way. She'd spent the evening with him. She'd felt both his passion and his control of it. She had no reason whatsoever to believe in him, and she might have imagined all sorts of things.

But he couldn't be guilty of murder.

How did she know that? She should run. Into the snow? No, back to his room. She should lock herself in. And she should—

"Whose murder?" she heard herself say.

"That's all that I'm telling you tonight," he said.

"But you can't just say something like that and go to bed!" she protested.

"I can, and I intend to," he told her firmly. "Now, if you don't mind—"

Her hand lay flat against the door to the guest room. He moved it so that he could close the door.

"But—but—"

He smiled icily at her. "Ah, but I *could* be a murderer, right? You've had your suspicions since you came. Especially when you thought I was going to shoot you with my shovel! Good night, Ms. Kennedy!"

He managed to shut the door on her. Kristin stood there in the hallway, shaking.

He was locking her out. She should be locking him out!

"Justin, how dare you scare the hell out of me like that!"

The door opened again and he stared at her hard. "I can't just scare you like that? Ms. Kennedy, may I remind you, you're the one outside here screaming at my door! Go to bed. Leave me alone for the night!"

The door closed firmly once again. And Kristin remained in the hall, stunned.

"Good night!" he snapped from behind the door.

She backed away. Then she turned and ran back down the hall, through the sitting room and into the bedroom. Closing the door behind her, she leaned against it, her heart hammering like wildfire.

But of course he wasn't coming after her. He had just thrown her out.

She slid the bolt on the door and went flying across the room. She curled into the bed, dragging the covers over her. She lay there numb and shivering.

Then she felt a bit like a fool. He didn't mean to murder her. If he'd wanted to hurt her, he could have done so any time. And he had not.

He just wasn't the type of man to be a murderer. How could she know that? She sighed. She didn't know. All that she did know was that she sensed something about him. He was a good man. And it wasn't just the chemistry between them. It was more than that. It was intuition. He couldn't have murdered anyone.

She didn't know anything about him. She should be nervous as all hell.

She needed to get some sleep. That was exactly what she needed. A really good night's sleep.

Sleep!

She'd never sleep. She might well be locked up in a house with a murderer.

No...

Intuition was not proof, she reminded herself. But still, she just knew that he couldn't be a murderer. It was absurd. After everything, she felt intuitively that he was a man who could be trusted.

Fool...

She closed her eyes. She felt the tension slowly ease away. She'd never, never sleep....

But she did sleep. A few minutes after her head hit the pillow, she was sound asleep.

A low-burning fire continued to crackle in the room's handsome fireplace, warming her.

Outside, the snowstorm raged on.

Justin was the one who couldn't sleep.

It wasn't because he wasn't in his own bed—he could sleep anywhere. He'd toured enough and taken enough business trips to be accustomed to sleeping in the worst possible locations.

And it wasn't the storm, or the past, or anything.

It was the woman.

The dark-haired beauty sleeping in his bed.

He closed his eyes, and he could see her still, the way she had looked in his kitchen. She had worn his white terry robe. Even rolled up, the sleeves had been floppy and too big. It had been a chaste garment on her, covering her from head to toe.

It had still been incredibly sexy.

Her hair had seemed so dark against it, deep, rich and dark with its satiny sheen. And those eyes of hers. Dovegray, steady, never seeming to falter. She stared at him with such an honesty about her. And her lashes were so long and rich and so demure....

She was really beautiful. He had known that from the first moment he saw her. Ah, yes, she was so very, very beautiful....

But he liked things about her, too. He liked the way she offered to cook. And he liked the way she did cook— her meal had been really delicious, the best he had tasted in a long, long time. And he liked her smile and the dimple in her cheek when she talked about her grandfather.

He had liked her in his living room, the way she had leaned against him, watching the old-time movie. She had looked good there, too.

She had felt good....

So good. When he kissed her, it had seemed that all the fires of hell had awakened inside his body. But those fires had been of the sweetest variety, the kind to awaken and restore.

And he had wanted so much more than that kiss!

Certain that she was the ultimate liar—an actress even finer than Myra had ever been!—he had still felt that searing attraction. Still wanted her with a passion stronger than any that he remembered.

Snowfire was about to open again. The reporters would all come crawling around again soon enough.

What the hell? If a really beautiful woman—who could cook, too—wanted to sleep with him for the story, why not get something out it? he asked himself wryly.

Because he wanted more from her, he realized. He wanted her to be telling him the truth.

And now, for the first time since she had arrived, he was beginning to be plagued with doubt. The amazement in her eyes when he had said the word *murder* had been so quick and so real, so damned real....

Could he have been wrong?

He turned over with a groan, determined to sleep. He wasn't going to lie awake all night because there was a stranger in the house.

But he was. He crawled out of bed and padded over to the window. The snow was falling with a fantastic vengeance, beating against the house.

He loved storms, the ferocity of the snow when it fell like this, the keening of the wind.

Somehow, they were soothing to his soul.

But nothing would soothe his soul tonight. He had meant to see just how far she would take a charade this evening. Instead, he had found himself pulling her into his arms.

And she had been so stunned when he mentioned murder.... Could she really have faked that?

She could be an excellent actress.

He pulled his jeans back on and opened his door and walked out into the dimly lit hall. From the hallway he entered his dressing room, and the bath. To his surprise, the knob of the door to his bedroom turned in his hand.

She hadn't locked it.

She'd probably locked the other door, and forgotten about the bath.

He shrugged, hesitated, then went into the bedroom.

He walked softly to the bed and looked down, and for a moment, a wry irritation seized him.

She was sleeping just as sweetly as a babe.

Still clad in his white robe, she was curled up on the bed. His pillow was beneath her cheek, and her flesh was cream and rose against it. Her fingers lay like red-tipped flowers over the darkness of his sheets. With her color restored to her, her lips, too, were a warm wine red against the black silk sheets.

She was a picture of innocence. Just like a princess in a fairy tale.

Life was no fairy tale, he reminded himself ruefully.

But just once, he wanted something good in it to be the truth.

He touched her cheek, and felt the softness of it. "Could you possibly, just possibly, be real, Ms. Kristin Kennedy," he whispered aloud. "Please, be real."

Little drumbeats began to pulse in his head. And then they began to play havoc with his body. Despite his shirtlessness, tiny beads of sweat were suddenly dripping down his chest.

He backed quickly away from her.

Gritting his teeth, he moved silently through the bathroom and down the hall to the guest room. Once there, he stripped off his jeans again and flung himself into the bed.

He had no reason to trust her. There was no reason to trust her at all.

Except that he wanted to.

He'd really be a fool if he did. He should have learned his lesson.

Sleep. He needed to get some sleep.

He closed his eyes tightly. He would not think about her anymore that night.

Sleep, damn it! he groaned inwardly to himself.

But it was a long, long time before he slept.

Chapter 4

Justin awoke to the subtle scent of enticing aromas coming his way. He frowned for a moment, then remembered that he had a guest in his house.

An intriguing guest.

He showered quickly, threw on a pair of jeans and hurried downstairs, barefoot, a denim shirt held slung over his shoulder.

She was an early riser. And she seemed to rise in a surprisingly fair disposition. Especially surprising after the way that he had left her last night.

"Good morning!" Kristin said as soon as she saw him in the doorway. "The electricity is still holding. Isn't it a miracle?"

"Umm. Quite a miracle." The bacon was sitting on a platter. He leaned across the island and stole a piece.

She was still wearing his white robe, but she, too, had been in the shower. Her hair was still wet, slick and damp and combed back from her face. She hadn't a stitch of makeup on and yet it just made her classic features and the huge dove-gray eyes more beautiful.

And he'd never known that the simple scent of soap on female flesh could smell quite so good.

You've no reason to trust her, he reminded himself. None whatsoever. She could be trying to seduce you into the scoop of the decade, and doing a very good job of it.

And then again...

She was still in the midst of making breakfast. The bacon on a platter, but she had the waffle iron going and she was rinsing strawberries in the sink. She had already brewed the coffee and poured the juice.

"Did you sleep well?" he asked her.

"Wonderfully. Except that I feel horrible about putting you out of your room. That's the most comfortable bed I've ever been on."

"Thanks."

He bit into another piece of bacon and then walked around the island to pour the coffee, dropping his shirt on the end of the counter as he did so. Her eyes flickered lightly over his bare chest and she flushed slightly. Then her eyes met his and she grinned.

"It's a good thing that the electricity is holding. I wouldn't want you to freeze."

"The heat here is oil." He grinned in turn, surprised and amused that she would think anything of a male with a bare chest.

And maybe she was even just a little uncomfortable. When he'd kissed her last night, he'd felt... fire. Something swiftly ignited and wild and sweet.

She wasn't the one growing uncomfortable, he determined. Watching her, damp and robed, and those dove-gray eyes on his, he felt something that could be damned quickly ignited himself.

He crunched another piece of bacon. Loudly. He was still suspicious of her. Very suspicious. After all, if he was a stranger in an even stranger house casting about the word *murder,* she should have been damned uneasy. And this morning, she was just as cool as could be.

"So." Still bare-chested, he leaned across the island counter. "You slept well."

"Like a log. After a while, that is," she admitted.

A smile slowly curved his lips. "Ah, the truth! So did you lie there wondering if you'd awaken when morning came?"

"No, I didn't. Not after a while."

"And why is that? I did tell you that I had been accused of murder. Weren't you surprised?"

"You know damned well that I was surprised."

"I know damned well you might be a very good actress."

Kristin exhaled with impatience. "Actress or no, Justin Magnasun, I obviously have a certain faith in you now. Because, as you might notice, I have preferred your company to crawling back into the snow."

"And why is that?"

She stopped what she was doing and stared at him, a brow arched, her tone just a bit on the superior side. "Because, granted, you were very rude when we met. Almost abusive. But then you did save me. And I was out cold for several hours. Then I awoke all in one piece. And you gave me your room, your things..."

"Murderers can be very polite, Ms. Kennedy."

"I never said that you were polite. I decided that a man who showed so much principle—despite his manners—couldn't be a murderer. Also, you're still a free man, walking around. If you went to court, a jury acquitted you."

He arched a brow, amused. "All that—when I really gave you nothing at all! So you thought this all through, and went to sleep. And you weren't just a little bit curious?"

"You know damned well that I was curious. I chased you down the length of the hall. You slammed a door in my face."

"I did, didn't I?" He sighed. "Hard to imagine that I could do that to a beautiful woman in nothing but a robe trying to get into a room where I was sleeping."

She cast him a quick gaze of rebuke, then lifted a waffle out of the iron.

"Thank you," she told him.

"What?"

"I said, thank you. You called me beautiful."

"Oh, and you've never heard it before?"

She smiled, her eyes on the waffle she lifted from the iron. "You certainly weren't impressed yesterday when we first met. You told me I could freeze in the snow before you'd let me near you."

"I hadn't had a good look at you then."

Her eyes shot to his as they both realized just how good that look had been. Justin lifted his hands quickly into the air. "I didn't mean that exactly the way that it sounded. I didn't mean that the way that it sounded at all. I meant...oh, hell! I meant that I really hadn't seen your face," he finished impatiently.

Her lashes, thick and sooty, fell over her eyes again. "Want to hand me a plate?"

He did so. And he poured the coffee. "Shall we eat in the sun room? Not that there's much sun."

The coffee mugs in his hand, Justin walked past the counter area and sat in one of the window seats. He set the mugs down on the ledge beside it, and patted the seat beside him. Kristin walked the plates over and set them down and started back into the kitchen.

"Where are you going?"

"To get the juice glasses."

"I'll get them."

She sat and he went for the juice. Then he returned and curled his feet beneath him, sitting cross-legged on the seat beside her. They were so close that his knee brushed her thigh. And it occurred to him that it was a nice way to be, that he was comfortable with her. He wanted her. He couldn't remember wanting a woman quite the way that he wanted her. But all the other things were nice, too. Seeing her face, sitting beside her. Watching her smile, and seeing that single dimple in her left cheek deepen. Just talking. Hearing the cadence of her voice.

Whoa! he told himself. Watch it. She can't be as innocent as she pretends to be.

He leaned back against the seat, looking out across the snow as he sipped his coffee.

She could even make a really good cup of coffee, he mused.

The snow was still falling. The storm hadn't lost one bit of its ferocity. From the window seat, though, it was beautiful. Dark, but beautiful, as the sky continued to roil in gray with the white flakes falling and falling.

She was watching him, he realized. He smiled. "I like storms."

"So do I. Except when I'm stuck in them."

"I didn't think that it was so miserable here."

She shook her head, smiling. "I'm not miserable here. But yesterday, I was terrified."

They were coming back around. Was she subtly questioning him? Or was it the natural fun of conversation?

He had thrown out the bait last night. He wanted her to question him.

He wanted to talk. To try to find out if there was any way at all to determine whether she might just be telling him the truth.

"Did I frighten you so badly?"

"You bet."

"That's right. When I was going to shoot you with my shovel."

She flushed. "You were pretty vehement."

He set down his coffee and picked up his plate. He bit into his waffle, then paused in his own chewing as he watched her mouth close over a strawberry.

A flash of heat sizzled through him. He wanted to be that strawberry.

He gave himself a serious mental shake. He couldn't go on like this. He started to chew again, and then he swallowed hard. And took another bite.

Kristin would never have guessed from his stony, immobile face that anything was disturbing Justin in the least.

She was concentrating herself on the way the man was disturbing her.

In her lifetime she had been to dozens of beaches. She'd seen male chests before. Lots of them. But there was something about this particular chest...

Maybe it was whom the chest belonged to. She wasn't sure. But from the moment he appeared that morning, he had started something inside her. Something warm that danced along her spine and into her limbs and into her heart. He was fresh from the shower, his hair damp, his cheeks cleanly shaven. His broad, sleek-skinned shoulders were well muscled, and she had a feeling that those muscles came from his love for this place, from chopping wood, from lifting and lugging, rather than from an exercise club. She liked his chest. A lot. It was a perfect chest. Beneath it his belly was lean and flat. Crisp dark curls of hair lay spattered over his chest, then narrowed to a dark swirl and disappeared beneath the waistband of his jeans....

And she had to quit staring.

She jerked her eyes back to his in sudden alarm, but for once he hadn't caught her. He was looking out the window, talking about the weather.

She moistened her lips. He was staring back at her again. His plate was empty and he unwound his long legs to take it into the kitchen. He reached for her plate. "Are you done?"

"Yes. Yes!" she agreed.

He took her plate and looked at the waffle remaining on it. His eyes met hers. "You're not very hungry."

"I ate."

"Yes. I noticed. Strawberries."

There was something curious about his gaze. Something that warmed her.

No, it made her downright hot....

"Ah...more coffee?" she asked. She leaped up, picked up their empty juice glasses and moved to the kitchen. He followed her, setting the plates in the sink. Kristin walked back for their cups and refilled them. When she turned from the coffeepot, he was right behind her.

"Well, we've had breakfast, and you haven't said a thing to me about last night."

She stared up at him. At the tension in his blue eyes.

"No," she whispered.

"Why not?"

"Well, you slammed a door in my face last night."

"That was then. This is now."

She flicked her tongue over her dry lips. How could she explain what she was feeling?

"Were you accused of murdering someone?"

"Yes," he said flatly. "But I can't believe you didn't figure that out by yourself last night. I thought that I might wake up to find you barricaded in my room. Instead, you're down here making breakfast. Why?"

"Not because I'm a reporter assigned to cover your case!" Kristin snapped out angrily. She would have pushed past him if she could have, but he was like a rock standing there before her. That same chest that had been so fascinating to her was barring her way.

"Then?" he demanded.

"If you were going to kill me, you could have done so already," she told him, aggravated.

"Yes, I could have." His lashes fell briefly over his eyes, then his gaze focused on her once again, hard as steel. "But maybe I like to draw things out. Maybe I want to entrap you in a web of trust and then . . ."

"Yes, maybe!" Kristin said icily. Then she exploded, "Why are you doing this to me?"

"Why would you trust me?"

"Because I thought it out. And I just don't believe you're that kind of a man. No, that's not really a reason, is it? There is no real reason! Trust isn't something that comes from knowing things!" she cried. "Trust is something that comes from intuition. I was frightened last night! You meant me to be frightened, and I was. But then I realized that I wasn't frightened of you—that I hadn't been, not since I awoke and discovered I was safe. You were honest with me. But that's not it, either. I do trust you, that's all. I don't believe that you could have murdered anyone."

She stopped speaking as if she had just run out of steam. He was still staring at her. Staring...taut and tense, a pulse raging against his throat. She wondered if he was even breathing.

Then he exhaled on a long breath. His eyes flicked over her.

"I didn't murder anyone. Is that enough for you?"

"What do you mean?"

"If that is all that I'm willing to tell you, will you trust me still?"

Kristin frowned, but she nodded slowly. "I already told you that I trusted you. That's not going to change."

She thrust his coffee mug at him. His fingers closed over it.

Setting her hand on his bare shoulder, she pushed past him.

Her hand seemed to burn.

She strode over to the sink with the plates. He was beside her again. "I'll do this," he told her curtly.

"No, I'll do it," she insisted.

"I said—"

"Do we always have to argue over dishes?" Kristin demanded, frustrated. At the moment, she just wanted him to keep his distance. She didn't like to argue with him. It made her want to touch him more.

"Let's just leave the damned dishes for a while."

"Fine."

They both stared at each other, their hands on their hips.

"What do you want to do?" she asked him.

He clenched his teeth.

There was no way to tell her what he really wanted to do. Fall on her. Right there, right now.

No. He wanted to shake her. He wanted to discover if she really believed everything she had said about trust.

And he desperately wanted to believe that his own overwhelming desire to trust in her was not a mistake, either.

"Music. I'll put on some music."

"That would be wonderful. You do that, and I'll do the dishes."

"Great."

He disappeared. A few minutes later she heard a soft, pleasant show tune echoing around her. Apparently he had speakers connected into the kitchen.

She set the last of the dishes on the drainboard and turned around and he was back in the room.

"What now?" he demanded. He was tense, like a tiger on the prowl. She felt that way herself.

She lifted a hand in the air. "I could go to your room. If I'm in your way."

"Lock yourself in?"

"That's not what I said!"

"You're not in my way."

"Then . . ."

"There's swimming," he murmured.

"I haven't a suit. Even if I could get to my car, I didn't expect to go swimming in winter." He was still staring at her. "I've nothing to wear."

"You don't—" he began, then he quickly, harshly corrected himself. "Yes, you do."

"Really, I—"

"Chess? Do you play?"

"Yes."

"Good. I'll get the board. You bring the coffee."

She decided to dump out the cold coffee and start over. She carried the two cups into the huge living room and found he had set up the chessboard on the ledge in front of the massive granite fireplace. He had dragged down the big pillows from the sofa for them to lean back against.

He didn't offer her the first move. He was white and he took it himself, breaking out his knight.

She was a more timid player. She started with a pawn. He followed suit. Then she realized that he was going to pull out his queen and send her into battle immediately. He'd eat her alive if she didn't begin to find some defensive strategy.

He was playing quickly. Too quickly, she decided. His weakness lay in his recklessness. If she played in a calm, considered fashion, she might do all right.

Fifteen minutes later, she had his bishop and his knight, but he had one of her rooks and three of her pawns and was relentlessly pursuing her queen.

"You don't give a lot of thought to your moves," she advised him primly.

He glanced at her quickly.

"I don't really feel like playing," he told her.

She stiffened. "Well, we don't have to play."

"Yes, we do. We need to do something. Anything that keeps the old hands and mind in motion. Move a piece."

"I can't play if you rush me!" she snapped. Then she saw a move she could make that would seize his queen. It was crafty and subtle. She hadn't used it in a long time because her cousin was the one who had taught it to her, and she almost never played chess except with Roger.

She smiled complacently. And started her move.

He watched the board at last. He was stretched out along the ledge, leaning upon one elbow. The firelight played a sensuous dance across his naked chest.

She lifted the terry robe from her neck and bit down on her lower lip. She wanted to cry out, demanding to know just what made this man so appealing. She didn't want to play chess, either. She didn't care if she listened to music or not, and she didn't give a damn about dishes. She wanted something to change the growing tension in her, something to ease the desire to reach out and touch his face. . . .

And that chest.

"It's your turn," he said. His gaze was on her. Sharply. On her eyes. Then upon her lips. Then lower.

She leaned over and moved a piece, taking his queen.

Startled, he sat up and stared at the board. She moistened her lips, her eyes downcast, and smiled.

"Where'd you learn that?" he demanded.

"Roger." She looked at him. The way he stared at her made her hurry up to explain, despite the fact that she didn't owe him any explanations. "My cousin, Roger Doria, taught me how to play. He's very good, and we're close."

The way he was looking at her made her keep talking, so nervous that she was suddenly a font of information. "I'm an only child in a huge family of cousins, so Roger rather took on the role of big brother to me. Would you please say something? Why are you staring at me like that?"

"Roger Doria!" he exploded.

She nodded, wondering what could create such a burst of emotion.

"Your cousin is Roger . . . Doria?"

She nodded. "Yes."

"Roger Doria of Warwick, Massachusetts?"

"Yes," Kristin said, amazed at the way he looked at her.

"Why didn't you tell me?"

"I did tell you! I told you from the beginning that I was on my way to see my cousin—"

"But you didn't tell me who!"

"You never believed me, and you never asked," she reminded him. She was starting to shiver. He was still so emotional, so...tense. What had Roger done to elicit such a response from this man? Roger was a nice guy, a really nice guy, and his wife, Sue, was a doll. "I—I take it that you know my cousin?"

She thought for a minute that he was going to throw the chess game into the air. Then he started to laugh.

"Yes, I know Roger."

"Did he do something to you? Is there anything wrong with Roger?" She was growing more and more confused by the minute.

He shook his head. She'd never seen his eyes so light. Nor his features so at ease.

"No, I like Roger. And Sue."

"Good." She stared at him, certain that he had lost some of his senses. And then she understood. He finally had proof that she was not lying. She gasped in anger. "Oh, I see now."

"What do you see?"

"You're willing to believe me now, you bastard!"

"Yes, I believe you. What's the matter with that? You just gave me something that I could believe—"

She shook her head, wondering herself at her sudden fury. "No one gave me any hard facts or evidence about you, Mr. Magnasun. I looked at you as a person, and I came to my own conclusions! Until this very minute, you never even thought of believing me! I was after you—for your wonderful story or scoop or whatever it is exactly that someone would risk life and limb to obtain. You didn't believe—"

"Oh, come on, now! I was giving you the benefit of the doubt! I wanted to—"

"The hell you were!"

He laughed, amused by her anger, suddenly very at ease, and very charming. "Honest! I was giving you the benefit of the doubt. It's just nice to know that Roger is your cousin."

"I was trusting you!"

"Well," he said softly, "maybe you just aren't quite as world-weary as I am yet."

Kristin stared down at the board again, a tense knot of emotion herself.

She moved her queen suddenly. "Check!"

He looked down at the board. His knight—obviously situated by her queen—moved the proper spaces to sweep up her threatening piece. "I think not."

She moved a bishop. "Check," she said again.

His rook took her bishop.

She was the one playing recklessly now, and she didn't know why. She only knew she couldn't continue sitting beside him calmly playing chess. He made her feel so very warm. And so very angry.

She wanted to jump away from him.

She wanted to move much closer to him....

She stared at the board, then moved a pawn.

He moved his knight again. "Check."

She studied the board. "Oh, all right, you've won."

"I didn't say checkmate. I said check."

"It's a stupid game, and I surrender."

He looked at her and smiled. "Do you?"

She gritted her teeth and exhaled. She saw the move that he had seen and made it. It didn't matter. She had thrown the game away. She was far too wound up to concentrate. She couldn't look at the board when she felt his eyes on her so.

And she kept staring at his chest, highlighted by the fire....

"Now it's checkmate," he said smugly.

"So it is."

"Do you want to play again?" he asked. His eyes were very bright in the firelight. His flesh was so very bronze...copper...glistening.

"No," she said.

She could almost feel his warmth. He wasn't touching her, but he seemed so close. And so tense again, watching her. Just watching her.

"Do you want to watch a movie?"

"No," she murmured.

And he smiled, slowly, ruefully. His eyes were a blaze of blue.

"Do you want to make love?" he asked softly.

She gasped, amazed that he could say something so outrageous and bold with such raw simplicity....

But then, it had been coming. It had been coming now for a long time.

His smile remained rueful, but his eyes were tense. The nearby fire seemed to crack and sizzle.

She should say no. It would be so simple. So easy. She should open her mouth and say no.

But she did want to make love. It was exactly what she wanted to do.

He shoved the chessboard aside and stood up. He walked around behind her, his eyes still on hers, his bare footsteps soft and silent, like the pad of a great cat.

His hands fell upon her shoulders as he knelt down there. His face was buried in the hair at her nape, and then she felt the softest touch of his lips against the lobe of her ear.

"It's a question," he told her softly. "You're allowed to say no."

Say no...

She barely knew him. He had admitted that he had been accused of murder.

And still, it was true. She trusted him.

Intuition.

Desire...

Soft, hot, wet kisses landed against her throat, teased her ear and moved along her throat once again. She sat still, pliable. And the sensations swept into her. Sweet sensations. The fire seemed to leap from the grate and enter inside her, yellow and gold, little laps and tongues of fire that entered her body where he touched her, and traveled through the length of her.

"Kristin...?" he whispered. The sound of her name was husky. Rough. It played against her flesh.

She turned and wound her arms around his neck. He lifted his face and she looked up into his eyes.

"Yes! That's exactly what I'd like to do," she told him. "Exactly."

He kissed her then. Kissed her with an explosion of the tension that had ripped between them all through the morning. Kissed her hard, and deep, seizing everything from her, and giving her a myriad of crystal sensation and emotion in return.

She'd never known anyone like him. Never felt anyone like him, this tense, this passionate. Creating sensation so strong that it seemed to touch a pinnacle that rose higher and higher.

His kiss alone did this. Delving into her, so deep into her mouth, and with such heat that she felt the fires blazing inside her again. His lips rose from hers, then touched them again, and again, his mouth forming and molding hers, finding a fascination in the same motions once again. His tongue just touched her lips, then swept into her mouth, seized her being, and then explored so lightly once again.

The white terry robe was falling from her shoulder. His kiss fell there. Moved along her neck. The robe fell farther and farther. She felt her bare flesh against his, and the sensation was wonderful, cool and hot all in one. She pressed her mouth against the pulse beating at his throat and teased it with her tongue.

The white terry robe fell discarded to form a pool by her knees. He swept her into his arms.

Her wide eyes met his.

"We're going upstairs," he said. "I don't want the first time to be on the floor."

She smiled, thinking that he had considered her sensibilities, and she was glad.

"It wouldn't matter," she told him.

"It would matter to me."

And maybe it did matter. She clung to him while he climbed the stairs, watching the blue of his eyes.

And she trusted him still. She shouldn't, but she did. And she knew that she was right.

Intuition . . .

She knew it was right to make love with him, too. He could be brash and rude, and he could be unerringly tender, too. She wanted him. Just as she was fascinated by him as a man, she wanted to know all of him.

They reached his bedroom, and he laid her down on the black silk sheets. The feel of them was even more exquisite against her flesh. So good. She nearly cried out at the touch of that silk, for her flesh suddenly seemed so very much alive.

She heard the rasp of his zipper and then his jeans were shed and he was back down beside her. He cradled her in his arms, and they rolled together in the tumbled silk. His lips touched hers again, and his kiss created all kinds of fires again, sweet little flames to leap and dance within her limbs.

His body pressed to hers, his fingers curled around hers, and she felt that she was sinking into a never-ending pool of black silk. The rough texture of his chest teased her breasts, the pressure of his hips just met her.

And between her thighs, she felt the decadent throb of his desire. Almost as reckless and arrogant as he could be himself, the pulse teased and elicited, no, demanded, a response.

But he kept on kissing her. Endlessly, as if he could not get enough of the taste of her lips. And when his mouth broke free from hers at last, it moved to her throat, hovering over the rampant beat of her pulse.

Then his eyes were fixed on hers, and he lifted his weight from her. He touched her lips with his forefinger, then drew a soft line from her mouth to her throat, and down lower, over her body. The soft draw of that single finger rounded her breast, and rounded it again. She inhaled sharply, feeling the response within her body, the hardening of her nipples. He drew a lazy circle with his finger once again, just brushed her lips . . . then teased the tip of her breast with just the tip of his tongue . . . before closing his mouth around it.

She whispered his name, her fingers threading into his hair. The feeling was so excruciating, so sweet. . . .

She didn't know if she tried to drag him from her, or hold him closer against her. It didn't matter. He was not leaving. Nor did he intend to hurry. His mouth lingered, his tongue lingered, touching, bathing, caressing that one taut peak until she thought she would scream. And while his lips played, his hands were not idle. His stroke moved down her body. Brushing her ribs, her inner arm. Cradling her hip. His fingers ... drifting over her back.

Then drawing circles. Low. Very low. Over her abdomen. Moving lower and lower until they brushed over the dark triangle at the juncture of her thighs. Teasing ...

More and more intimately. His soft, gentle probe moved against her, within her. She gasped at the sudden invasion and boldness of it, tensing, nearly blinded by the new sensation. And then he brought with it a startling rhythm while the searing white heat of his mouth continued to caress her breast.

She no longer whispered his name. It exploded from her lips, and suddenly he was rising above her again. His eyes seemed to tear into hers, passionate, vibrant, demanding. And perhaps questing, still ...

Then they raked over the length of her. And he whispered her name. Then he groaned, and his face came against her throat and he said her name again, and again.

She curled her arms around him, holding him close. "Please..." she murmured. Her fingers curled into his hair again. Ran down his back. His back was good. It felt so good ... just to touch.

She felt his hand on her again. Flat this time, his palm moving down the length of them, between them. Touching the soft damp petals of her sex, his fingers moving intimately again. Then his eyes were on hers, and he entered her body. Slowly. She trembled with a jolt of searing sensation just as he touched her....

And she trembled again as he moved, his body sinking deeper and deeper into her own. The room careened around her, and she was suddenly aware of nothing but the shaft of his body, in her, stroking within her, caressing....

Some soft sigh escaped her, an expulsion of breath. She felt that movement as he held himself above her, coming in, slowly withdrawing, coming in again.

And all her senses were alive and vibrant, and concentrated upon him, upon the feel of his body against hers. The world was eclipsed.

Outside, the snow fell and the storm raged. And inside, the fires burned. New blazes leaped to life with each moment that passed.

Kristin cried out and threw her arms around him, pulling him down to her. Her teeth and tongue moved over the lobe of his ear, teased his neck. She bit lightly into his shoulder, then kissed the spot, clinging to him, swept within the growing fever pitch of his motion. They rolled upon the silk, their flesh so pale against the blackness of the silk.

The silk encompassed her. She met his eyes again as he pressed her back into it. And then she couldn't move, she couldn't touch him, she could only meet his eyes....

And feel his body and her own as he pumped in a sudden, reckless, wild tension. The room seemed to spin. Desire was bubbling within her. It was delicious, and it was anguish. She was desperate to reach the crest. She undulated to his slightest move, her hips rising against his. She choked out his name, then cried it out. He caught hold of her hands, pressing them down, too. And his fingers entwined there with hers while he thrust ever more deeply against her.

And then it seemed that he exploded within her, rocketing against her. And the touch, hot and sleek, the feel of the searing seed of his body, entered her like a taste of mulled wine. And the pinnacle of her own fulfillment burst upon her, like stars in the black velvet of a winter night. The feelings washed over her. Cascaded down and over her, so wonderfully rich. Blackness seemed to surround her....

She closed her eyes, shaking as the aftermath of her climax brought tiny new sensations, softer and softer, sweeping through her. He lifted his weight from her, regretfully. She trembled again as he pulled himself from her body.

He lay down beside her. She opened her eyes, and the world was still black.

It was a world of black silk....

She would never, never forget the feel of it.

He touched her chin, and she lifted her eyes to his. He leaned down and touched her lips lightly, tenderly with his own. Then his blue gaze swept the length of her, and a slow smile curled into his lips.

"This was a hell of a lot better than a game of chess."

A flush quickly colored her cheeks, and he laughed and kissed her again.

"Justin—" she began.

"I didn't tell you that you were exceptionally beautiful, did I?" he asked her huskily.

She smiled, lowering her lashes. He really could be an extraordinary host. Even here, he was trying to make her feel comfortable. But she wasn't uncomfortable. She had come here with him more than willingly.

But his eyes were dancing now, and he rose above her again, careful to balance his weight as he straddled her.

"I mean you are really, really beautiful on black silk," he said huskily.

"You're rather beautiful on black silk yourself," she told him. She reached out to touch him again. There was so much that she liked about him.

That chest...

That great, dark furred chest with its ripple of muscle and its delightfully rough texture. And his legs, tightly molded thighs and calves. She liked his hands, long-fingered, bold, talented.

She smiled wickedly. "Your eyes are just great against black silk."

He arched a brow. "Really."

"Really."

"You are an incredible woman."

He seemed serious. And so sincere. And it mattered so very much to her.

"Do you say that... often?" she asked him. She wanted the question to be light. She hadn't asked for promises. Neither had he. They had just needed to come close to each other.

But the closer they came...

The more it seemed to matter.

"I've never said it to anyone before."

"Never?" she whispered.

"Never," he promised.

He lifted her hand to his lips and kissed just the very tip of her fingers. Then he drew her finger lightly into his mouth. Just the tip. And he moved his tongue over it. She caught her breath, realizing that she was squirming beneath him again.

"Admit it," he demanded. "This was a lot better than chess."

"It was a lot better than chess," she told him.

"Good," he said. Then he lowered himself slowly against her. "Want to play again?"

"Chess?" she asked.

He didn't answer her, but she knew that he didn't have chess in mind at all.

Because he kissed her...

And the game that he meant to play was reengaged.

Chapter 5

The next morning, the electricity gave up at last.

Justin had a small battery-operated television, so they were able to find out what the storm was doing. New England had come to a screeching halt as the blizzard raged on.

"It will be days before you can get out of here," Justin told Kristin, pleased.

She laughed, pleased herself, and amazed that she could feel that she had found a little piece of heaven here, captive with a man who had once seemed so determined to rid himself of her whatever the cost.

It was a fool's paradise, she reminded herself. And in all of her life, she had never done anything like this. Trusted quite so easily.

Fallen quite so deeply for a man. For a total stranger.

But she didn't want to think about that. She didn't want to think about anything but the relationship between the two of them. She'd never felt like this before.

But then she'd never been in a situation like this before. Isolated as they were, some things just seemed understood.

They had both napped, awakened, sat in the whirlpool together, talked lazily and made love again. And then Justin had been hungry, but they hadn't had a lot of energy, so they had eaten fruit and cheese before the living room fire. And then they'd made love there, with Kristin protesting that he hadn't wanted to do so there before.

"Ah, but that was only the first time!" He laughed. "We've a whole house to go through now."

Later they'd gone back up to Justin's room and the black silk sheets, and they'd fallen to sleep there. Kristin had awakened once to find him watching her. And he had drawn a pattern around her lips with his finger, and asked her what she was doing on her own.

"Never married? It's difficult to believe. Some young fellow must have set out to snare you."

She smiled, but she winced at the same time. "I was married. For three years, but it seems like a long time ago now."

"What happened?"

"It wasn't so much 'what' happened as it was 'who' happened," she said with a note of irony. "I was very young when I married. And I was planning on college, but he was already enrolled, and so I was going to work. I worked very hard, and he started having a lot of fun. I imagine I was rather trusting for a while, but then I managed to get off early one night and when I came home, he was entertaining. In our apartment."

"What did you do?"

"I think I walked most of Boston at two a.m. I never went back." She smiled. "I ran home to Mother. My parents are great. No questions, just a place to stay."

"And that was it? You never discussed the situation with your husband?"

She shook her head. "I was shattered. There was nothing to discuss. I'd never have trusted him again. And if you can't trust someone, you can never relax, you can never be happy." She frowned, moving her fingers over the black sheets. "I don't know if we were ever really in love with each other. Deeply in love. We were so young back then. Sometimes I think that we were both in love with the idea of being in love."

"But you trust me," he murmured.

She smiled, her eyes very wide as she watched him. "I never felt the entire world should be condemned because I had a bad marriage. I've known far more fine and trustworthy people—men and women—than I have known those who are cruel or treacherous."

"Well," he said bitterly, "I have not had that experience."

"You don't seem to trust anyone."

"People are always just looking out for themselves. Especially women ... and reporters."

Guilt seemed to singe her heart. She had to tell him the truth about herself. She just needed the right time to do so. She couldn't just tell him. He was too bitter when it came to a point of trusting anyone.

But she had trusted him! When she should have been frightened of him, when the things that he had decided to tell her were just so damning.

Against all odds, she trusted him. She wished that she could have the same in return.

He was studying her, perched up on an elbow. "You took your own name back?"

"What?"

"Your own last name. After your marriage. You took it back?"

She nodded. "It was important for me to do so. I quit working and stayed home and went on to Holy Cross. Maybe I was trying to erase the whole thing, I don't know."

"You know, Ms. Kennedy, you may be too trusting an individual," he told her.

She shook her head, smiling slightly. "I'm trusting, but I don't trust just anyone."

"You trusted me. After I tried to shoot you with a shovel."

She smiled, but said simply, "I trust you."

"You made a mistake before."

"My instincts have been finely honed since then."

He had smiled and taken her into his arms....

And now, with the night behind them and morning on them again, Kristin still felt like a honeymooner. They had breakfasted on toast made over the fireplace, and now they were both curled on the sofa, idly watching the blaze. Candles gleamed from silver sconces, while outside the day remained dark. Time had little meaning. They were warm inside. Kristin set down her cup and leaned her face against Justin's shoulder. She didn't ever want to leave, she realized.

And she still didn't know anything about him.

He shifted suddenly, looking down into her eyes. "You still haven't asked me any questions," he said.

"I don't dare. You'll bite my head off and throw me out into the snow."

"Still think that I would do that?" he teased.

"Yes!" she told him flatly.

"So you've really taken me on trust alone. After everything," he murmured.

She nodded, smiling, then her smile faded. "I don't know what happened, but it must have been awful for you. What happened? Why were you accused?"

He stared at her for a long time. "You really don't know who I am?" he asked.

She shook her head. "You're not really Justin Magnasun?"

"Yes, I am Justin Magnasun," he said wryly. "But it's not the name that the world knows me by. Well, the theater-going world, that is."

Intrigued, Kristin pushed against his chest and stared at him. "Who are you to the theater-going world?"

"Jon Mountjoy."

She gasped, jerking up and gazing at him with disbelief, and then total understanding.

Jon Mountjoy...

Oh, she didn't know the details, but she knew all about the scandal. He'd been arrested for the murder of his wife, Myra Breckenridge, the beautiful—and hot, hot, hot!—star of stage and screen.

Out at his country house...

Here. Right here. He was supposed to have killed her here.

"Oh, my God!" Kristin breathed.

"Still trust me?" he taunted.

"Yes, I do."

"It's so damned hard to believe," he said softly, touching her hair.

She shook her head, feeling an overwhelming tenderness sweep through her. "It's not hard!" she answered equally softly.

"I've been burned pretty badly."

"So have I."

He shook his head, watching her still. "Not like I've been burned," he assured her.

Jon Mountjoy...

If she'd even given it some thought, she might have recognized him. Although playwrights didn't make headlines in the scandal magazines as movies stars did, Jon Mountjoy had been in the public eye often enough. His first hit play had appeared off-Broadway when he had been a student at Columbia in New York City. His next play hit Broadway, not only to rave reviews but to warm audience responses. Kristin could remember a review she had read of one of his plays a few years ago: "Mr. Mountjoy gives us everything, a gamut of emotions. We laugh, we cry, we strive along with his characters, flesh-and-blood people with real pathos and humor."

She'd seen pictures of him. But he'd always been turning away, avoiding the camera. And in the quick flashes taken at Broadway openings he was always dressed in elegant tuxes.

Not in jeans and flannel. Or in nothing at all.

Kristin had always assumed he was a much older man.

She remembered seeing glimpses of him on television during the trial, entering or leaving the courthouse. He'd never had a single comment for the media, and that had probably angered a number of reporters, and in turn they had been harsh on him.

And they had painted Myra Breckenridge as a being far more beautiful than any mortal could have been.

But she was beautiful . . . Kristin thought.

"I can almost see the gears of your mind in motion, Ms. Kennedy," he said.

Once again he was shirtless, barefoot, clad only in his jeans. He moved back, leaning against the far side of the couch, his bare feet upon it, his hands folded idly between his knees. Again, his naked flesh seemed very bronze in the firelight. Shadows of flame fell across him, darkening his features. He appeared very comfortable, but she had the feeling that he could move in a flash if he so desired. He wasn't comfortable at all. He was wary. And he was watching her for any response whatsoever.

"You do recognize the name?" he asked.

She nodded. "Of course. I love your plays. *Midnight and Lace* was my favorite. I never saw *Snowfire*—"

She broke off. *Snowfire* had just opened when Myra Breckenridge died. She had been the leading lady, and the play had closed after her death.

His lip curled into a wry smile. She wondered how she could have spoken so foolishly.

"I wasn't really asking what you thought of my work," he said dryly. "And I'm sure my name is far more familiar because of the scandal than because of my work."

Kristin shook her head, irritated. "I would have known your name one way or the other," she insisted.

He jumped up and started to prowl the room like a cat. He paced the floor behind the couch, then strode over to the granite mantel, leaned an elbow against it and stared into the flame. "You're a theater lover?" he asked, a casual, polite tone to his voice.

"Yes."

He spun around. "You're not afraid. You're really not afraid? I'm supposed to have strangled her with her scarf and my bare hands, you know."

Kristin stared at him levelly. "You were acquitted of murder."

"Lack of evidence. That's not entirely reassuring to the bulk of the population."

Kristin waved a hand in the air. "This all happened at least four years ago—"

"Five," he corrected her.

"What difference does it make!" Kristin snapped. "You said you didn't do it."

"You're taking me at my word that simply?" he asked softly.

Taking him at his word that simply...

Yes, she had done that since she came here. She had awakened in a strange bed—on black silk sheets, no less—naked and confused, and she had believed him then. She believed in him.

A cold shiver ripped through her.

She should be frightened, she told herself.

She was snowbound with this man, caught here in this house.

And they had said that he strangled his wife with his bare hands.

They were strong hands. She had felt them often enough now. She knew them very well. They were long, strong hands, with long tapering fingers. Broad at the palm. Very powerful.

But he wasn't a murderer. She was convinced of that.

She shrugged, watching him. "Want to tell me what happened?"

He grinned. "Sure. Just so long as you're not going to write all about it."

She wasn't, of course she wasn't. But a sudden searing guilt tore through her and it was hard to keep her smile. She must tell him the truth about herself. She should have done so sooner. She just couldn't do it now. "I—well, I poured out my heart to you," she said lightly.

He was quiet for a moment. "I'm not quite sure that it compares to murder," he responded harshly.

"My life wasn't as important as yours?" she snapped. "You know, your ego is quite incredible." She was suddenly terribly nervous, and anxious to be away from him. No matter how smoothly they seemed to be going along, his temper could suddenly lash out.

There wasn't anywhere to go—except out into the snow. But Kristin was both hurt and uneasy.

And if he knew what she did for a living...

Would he ever believe that it was just a coincidence?

"Don't," she told him, her tone as harsh as his. "Don't tell me a damned thing, I don't want to know."

She whirled around. She wasn't sure where she was going—just somewhere away from him for the moment.

"Kristin!"

She ran for the stairs, his bathrobe flapping around her knees.

He caught her at the base, whirling her around to face him. "I'll tell you—"

"No!" She stared at his hand, not bothering to wrench away from him.

"Then damn it—"

"I just don't want to be around you!" she cried.

His fingers tightened. She never could have escaped him if he wanted to hold her.

But he let her go. She turned and ran swiftly up the stairs and into his room. Sitting cross-legged at the foot of the bed, she stared into the flames. Then she fell back on the sheets.

Jon Mountjoy...

She shivered. He hadn't been exaggerating. It was this month's big story. The story of the year maybe.

Because *Snowfire* was opening on Broadway once again. She closed her eyes, trying to remember the exact date. Before Christmas, she thought. Some of the news-based programs at night were already doing spots on Myra Breckenridge, beautiful Myra, cut down in her prime....

And she had been beautiful. Tall, slim, golden blond, with huge blue eyes. She and Justin had been in love. Deeply in love.

At first, Kristin reminded herself with a frown. They'd been separated at the end. Right before *Snowfire*.

She shivered, and pulled the robe more tightly about her. She stood up and walked to the fire and warmed her hands before it. Then she walked over to the mirror and stared at her reflection. Gray eyes framed by black lashes, and a lean face framed by thick dark hair. There wasn't a speck of makeup on that face.

She didn't begin to compare with Myra Breckenridge.

"Oh!" She gasped out loud, realizing that she was jealous of a ghost.

Ripples of restlessness tore up and down her spine. She started to pace the room.

Why was she here?

Maybe she was afraid. Now that she knew who he was, was she afraid of him? How was he going to feel when he found out the truth about her?

He had to come to trust her as a person. Then maybe she could make him understand.

"Kristin!"

The bedroom door was suddenly flung open. Justin's fingers were wound into fists at his sides. His tension was visible in the strain that knotted his muscles and corded his neck.

"Kristin!" he said again, more softly this time.

She stared across the room at him, then she suddenly ran to him, pitching herself into his arms.

I love you....

The words were right on the tip of her tongue as she clung to him, delighting in the feel of his body against hers. But she couldn't say words like that. It could still be argued that she barely knew him.

His arms clasped her warmly. He lifted her from the floor and held her tightly. Then he let her slowly slip back to her feet.

"If you're afraid of me, if you're ever afraid of me, I'll leave you alone," he swore raggedly.

"I'm not afraid."

"Then why—"

"I did rather pour out my whole life to you," she told him. "And you made light of it."

He smiled ruefully. "I didn't say that your life wasn't every bit as important as mine. But confessing to a failed marriage is not exactly on a par with murder."

"You didn't confess to murder," she told him.

"You believe that I didn't murder her?"

She smiled. "I know that."

"How do you know that?"

"I trust you."

"You're right. I didn't murder her. Do you want to hear about it?"

"Only if you want to tell me?"

"I think that I do," he said softly. "Kristin—I can't help it, I'm sorry. I really do hate reporters, all reporters. And until you mentioned Roger... Well, I don't really know how to trust anyone on instinct. I've never been able to do so before. I thought you were that little witch on the phone who had been so determined to see me.

"Kristin, when I was first acquitted, I was besieged here by the press. I had given up my apartment in Manhattan and moved out here full-time, and so they all followed me to the country. And one damned man— from a highly respected paper!—was in such a hurry to beat someone else to me that he ran over my dog. The whole crop of locusts took off then, but it was too late for poor Jugs." His eyes were like steel, but Kristin could see pain in their depths. "So you see, I'm afraid that I'm not very reasonable."

Her mouth had formed into an O.

She should have told him, but now she wondered if she ever could.... Guilt ripped through her.

"Let's go back downstairs," Justin said softly.

Tell him.

Are you crazy? Not now!

She had to make him believe in her!

He caught her fingers and entwined them in his own. She followed him silently downstairs to the living room, where the fire was burning the most brightly. She found herself sitting again and him pacing again.

"Were you in love with her? Terribly in love with her?" Kristin asked.

He cast her a quick glance, then gazed at the fire and shook his head.

"Once...I suppose. I was taken in by her beauty. But that was when we first met. I was several years younger than she was, and I think that fascinated her. She was thirty then, and I have never seen anyone in my life so obsessed with age. Maybe she had depended on that beauty of hers too much. Maybe she never enjoyed it, really, because she was always so certain that it would fade." He shrugged and gazed around the living room.

"She never liked this place. She came out twice while it was being built and promised me that she would never tuck herself away in the country—in the boondocks, the sticks!—like this. I'd never asked her to tuck herself away, I just loved the countryside, and I loved this area. I loved the forests and the quiet. It was a wonderful place to write."

Roger had said much of the same thing to her when he and Sue moved out here. Kristin could understand it herself from the few times she had been able to drive out to visit him and Sue. The countryside was beautiful. In fall, with its profusion of colors. In winter, with a sparkling coat of snow. And in summer, with an endless canopy of green. An ever-changing land. Kristin loved it herself.

Myra Breckenridge had not.

And she had died here.

"But you were married—"

"Not happily. Not from the moment we said our vows. I'm not sure that she really intended to do it. Nor that I did, not really. We met at the opening of *Promises to Keep*. She'd asked a mutual friend to introduce us. She'd been out in Hollywood before that, but her last movie had been a hopeless flop. We met. We were with a group and we wound up at Sardi's, and the entire party drank too much. She was vivid, colorful. I'd been working too hard. She was a breath of fresh air. The next week, we planned a trip to Las Vegas. Just to gamble, see the shows, have some playtime. And we were having fun. Myra could charm when she wanted to. We began to talk about the way our lives coincided, and then we were talking about marriage, and the excitement of it seemed overwhelming. And there we were in Vegas. Marriage was as easy as taking in a show. Not that I didn't know what I was doing. I did. I was in love with one of the most beautiful women in the world. And I think she was in love with me, too, then. As much as Myra was capable of being in love.''

''Then what happened?'' Kristin asked softly.

He shrugged. ''Playtime ended. I'm a writer. It's not just what I do, it's part of being me. I hate the spotlight—Myra loved it. No, she needed it. She couldn't live without it. We were barely together before we drifted apart. Myra was a real party person. She'd travel somewhere, ostensibly on business, and I'd hear tales about her that would make your toes curl.

''I flew out to Hollywood to see her when she was supposed to be working. I didn't catch her in the act of anything, but I knew what she'd been up to. I do have some pretty good friends in this business. They managed, one way or another, to keep me up-to-date. They didn't want me hurt. But by then I didn't love her enough to be hurt. So I saw Myra. I told her it was over. She cried—she was the ultimate actress. But I went back to New York and she stayed in Hollywood—and she made another bomb of a movie.''

''I remember it,'' Kristin murmured. ''The comedy. It really was terrible.''

''Her agent told her to go back to Broadway. But she was getting older, so she couldn't play an ingenue anymore, and there just didn't seem to be anything for her to sink her teeth into.''

He exhaled, and Kristin felt a touch of the sorrow he had felt for Myra Breckenridge. He might have fallen out of love with her, but he had never ceased to care for her.

''She came to me. Her life was in a shambles. I suggested that she might try to cut down on some of the drinking and the drugs. She told me that she needed them to get by, and I told her that she didn't. If she would just come out here to the country with me, I could guarantee that I could clean her up out here. But she refused. She wanted a play, but not badly enough to stay out here. I wanted to help her. She was still my wife, even if there was nothing left between us.

''So I wrote *Snowfire.* We had our big opening, and the play was such a success that it was a phenomenon. Myra was so thrilled that she asked everyone to a party on the dark day. A party here—in the sticks. She looked well, she was feeling wonderful, and she was even off a lot of the booze and the pills. She chartered a plane, and we all flew out here. We had the food catered and the place festooned with banners. There had been a blizzard a few weeks before, and the snow was beautiful here, really beautiful, white, just touched with ice. The type of snow that glitters all kinds of colors in sunlight and moonlight. Dazzling. Snowfire. And Myra died in it.''

''Why did they accuse you? You weren't alone out here!'' Kristin said indignantly.

He laughed softly. ''My defense lawyers weren't so enthusiastic! I thank you. I suppose the police always look to the husband. Everyone knew we were at odds with each other.''

"But you'd written a play for her!"

He nodded. "Yes, well, I wasn't on trial for first-degree murder. They didn't think I'd planned it ahead of time, just that I'd done it in a jealous rage." He hesitated a moment. "And we had a monstrous fight that night. I told her I was moving out here for good. She made a dramatic statement in front of the whole party about me wanting to kill her. And she kicked Jugs. I grabbed her and told her I would kill her if she kept it up."

"Oh." Kristin murmured. Her mind was working. She shook her head, staring at the fire herself. "If you didn't kill her, Justin, then someone did."

"Yes, I pointed that out to the authorities when I was acquitted. They didn't pursue it."

"Why?"

Again he hesitated. Then he sighed. "Kristin, they acquitted me because of lack of evidence. But I don't think the police ever once thought I was innocent. Obviously, they still think I did it."

"What about you?"

He shrugged. "What is there to pursue? Don't you see, there isn't any hard evidence. Someone here that night killed her, but I'll be damned if I know who it was," he said, tension and anger rife in his voice.

"Who was here?" Kristin interrupted.

He shrugged. "The four cast members—that would be Myra, Roxanne Baynes the ingenue, Jack Jones the male lead, Harry Johnston the character actor. Let me see, Artie Fein, Myra's agent was here. And Christina Anderson, my agent. The maid who had been hired to cater the party. And Joseph Banks, the film critic, and his wife. But the two of them never left the sofa you're sitting on, I'd swear it. The others . . . well, we were all wandering around the house. Myra just wandered outside sometime during the evening. I was already outside, down by the road. We had just quarreled, and I had wanted to be alone. It was when I was coming back to the house that I found her. In the snow. And then everyone found me there with her."

"Then what?"

"Well, I called the sheriff, of course. And he came out, and Myra was taken into the next town, we don't have a morgue here. They questioned all of us. Everyone was hysterical, but they all agreed that I'd threatened Myra. I was arrested. They let me out on bond—there were people who thought that Myra deserved to be strangled. The play closed, of course, and the press was all over me. I came to trial, but I was acquitted. So I moved back here, and eventually people forgot and the press left me alone. Then what?

"I felt sorry for myself for at least two years. Then I started writing again. Two years ago an old business associate came to me and told me he wanted to produce the new play I had finally finished, but first he wanted to reopen *Snowfire*. It was a good play, the law had said I was innocent, and holing myself up in the country was insane. He'd always been a good friend. I finally agreed." He hesitated strangely.

"And then...?"

"And then I began to be hounded by all sorts of media people again. Like the woman who called the other morning insisting that she was coming out. The one I told not to come here."

"The one you were convinced was me?" Kristin asked softly.

He waved a hand in the air. "She was some kind of a free-lance reporter."

A brick seemed to land in the pit of Kristin's stomach.

"Did you ever think that it might be a good thing to reopen it all, hash it all out?" Kristin asked him.

"Not that way," he told her.

"No, no, listen to me," she persisted. "If you spoke to someone, if you told it all to them, like you just told me, it might make the police get serious about investigating the case again. Maybe they'd find the real murderer."

"How are you planning on having them manage that now?"

"Well, there must be something to follow—"

"She was strangled with her own long red scarf. That's what killed her. There were no fingerprints that weren't already everywhere. The killer was wearing gloves—everyone was wearing gloves, it was winter."

"But who wanted to kill her?"

"Me—according to everybody, including the police," Justin said.

"Don't you want to find out!" Kristin cried in frustration.

"Yes, I want to find out," Justin said with a sigh. "But it would have been impossible. Everybody was all over the place. It was a party, Kristin. People weren't staring at one another all the time. And Myra could be a wicked, wicked witch when she wanted, so anyone could have wanted to kill her. I think all of us had probably quarreled with her at one time or another. I did think of Artie—but she made big money for him. She might have been slipping, but even for a bomb of a movie, her name could bring in some big money. I wondered about her leading man Jack Jones—"

"There! That's it. They were having an affair!"

"An affair is hardly enough for murder—"

"If she exposed him?"

"Who would care?"

"Then what about the other man?"

"Harry Johnston. He'd worked with Myra before. They were casual friends. She made him look very good onstage. He liked her."

"The girl?"

"Roxanne? Why would she want to kill Myra? The play was her big break."

"Oh, I don't know!" Kristin said with frustration. She cast him a quick glance. "You keep telling me why they wouldn't want to kill her. But there is a reason out there, Justin, that someone did want to kill her."

"Not me?" he asked with a soft smile.

She shook her head. "Not you."

He left the fireplace and came toward her, catching her hands, pulling her up into his arms. "You're really beautiful, do you know that?"

"Thanks," she said softly. "Not exactly Myra Breckenridge—"

"She couldn't hold a candle to you," he said softly, touching her cheek. "Myra needed paints and lights to become beautiful. She needed the sound of applause. And when you stripped her down, she was just a shallow child. A lost one. I pitied her. But you, Ms. Kristin Kennedy, you're really beautiful. From those dusky gray eyes of yours to the heart and the soul, you're beautiful." He brushed her lips with a light kiss, and met her eyes again. "We've had enough of true confessions for the moment, don't you think?"

Now it was her turn to make a confession. She needed to tell him that she was a reporter. Not *the* reporter, but a reporter.

She felt so damned guilty! And she wasn't guilty of anything! It's just that . . .

It was just that she was a reporter. She couldn't tell him now. Not now. It wasn't the right time. She had to tell him soon.

Before the snow stopped flying.

But she had come to trust him, and she wanted him to trust her, too. She wanted him to keep his arms around her as he was doing now. She wanted to feel his eyes upon her as they were now, endlessly blue, and tender.

He wasn't really waiting for an answer from her. "Ever been swimming in the snow?" he asked her.

"Swimming in the snow?" she repeated.

"Well, not swimming in the snow," he said with a laugh. "Swimming in water, while it's snowing."

She shook her head. He caught her hand and drew her across the room to the handsome glass doors that led out to the enclosed patio and pool. He pulled them open, and ushered her out to the white brick patio. The pool was tiled in shades of turquoise. The whirlpool at the end danced and cascaded and created a fall that rushed into the full body of the water.

Behind her he stripped off his jeans. Then his hands were on her shoulders, slipping off the terry robe. It fell sensually to her feet.

But he didn't touch her again. He walked on by her to the water. Naked and sleek, he dived in. She watched his bronze body cut across the water. He surfaced and looked back to her.

"It's warm as toast," he promised.

Kristin felt a soft current of air sweep by her. Warm. Or maybe the current was within her. She'd never stood on a patio like this . . . naked.

She'd never been skinny-dipping.

With him, it seemed right. And even knowing that they wouldn't end it with skinny-dipping seemed right, too. She'd never felt so comfortable, so at ease.

Nor so very warmed, by such very simple things.

He was watching her, his eyes touching hers, then slipping down her body.

With a soft little cry she ran across the brick and leaped from it, making a clear clean dive into the water. She swam across the width of the pool until she reached him where he rested his head upon the ledge. His arms closed around her. The stroking of his hands combined with the whisper of the water, sleek and sexy. Her legs tangled with his. She felt the roughness of the hair on his.

And her eyes widened as she felt the size of his sex between.

He grinned lazily, and pulled her against him. He wasn't in any hurry. He pointed up at the glass enclosure that shielded them from the outside. The snow was still falling. Landing upon that glass roof, then sliding down the slopes of it.

And outside, the snow was piled high. High and white. Steam rose off the water, a steam that gave credence to its warmth.

Nothing like the warmth of being in his arms.

"Like it?"

"Umm," she murmured. But then she shot away from him, enjoying the water. She swam the length of the pool, and waited for him in the shallows.

She'd come to him.

It was his turn to come to her.

And he did. Hard clean strokes brought him to her. He backed her against the tiled wall. And then he lifted

her high in his arms, and when he brought her down
again, it was to impale her.

A startled "Oh!" escaped her.

His eyes met hers and he laughed. She wound her
arms and legs around him, and he began to move, the
pulse and thrust of his body seeming to grind ever more
deeply into her.

The steam rose around them. His lips caught hers, and
he kissed her endlessly. Wet and slick, their bodies fused
and met and slid sensually against each other. The steam
seemed to swirl and tumble, and the reckless need tore
through her until a blinding brilliance came to burst
through the gray of the day, shattering her with a heat
like that of the sun, filling her. . . .

Filling him.

She laid her cheek against his shoulder, gasping for
breath, feeling the aftermath of her climax softly tremble through her . . . again, and again.

He held her close in his arms, and kissed her cheek.

"I could really get to like this," he whispered softly
against her ear.

"This . . . ?"

"Being with you."

He pulled her into his arms and kissed her again.
Slowly. His lips parted from hers. Just a breath.

"Being with you," he repeated huskily.

There was no other world, Kristin thought. No other
world at all.

They were encased in a paradise of snow, and there
was nothing that could come between them.

Nothing at all.

Nothing except who she really was.

Nothing except for the melting of that snow. . . .

Chapter 6

The days while the blizzard raged and the fires inside the snowbound world blazed were simply paradise. Kristin could not remember ever being so comfortable with one person. Perhaps comfortable wasn't the word, because Justin could be disturbing, too. He could come suddenly from behind her and sweep her off her feet, and comfort would be the very last thought in her mind. He could rouse her to heights, excite her as no other man could. But there was wonder, too, in the way he simply held her. There was magic in the darkness when they just sat before the fire and watched the flames turn color and listened to the snap and crackle of the logs.

She didn't want it to end. She was a captive of the storm, but a willing one, in an exquisite playground. They managed to make it through several games of chess. There were a few that they didn't quite get through, but that didn't matter. He was easy to laugh with, Kristin quickly discovered. Easy to be with.

They spent time reading, for he had an extensive library. She was fascinated with his office, with the original manuscripts of his plays. And in the far rear of the house was a game room with a billiard table and Ping-Pong table, and there was always the pool.

She loved the pool. Loved it.

She loved to sink back into his arms while the warm water rushed around them and the pale steam rose, fogging the glass enclosure. But beyond the fog she could still see the world outside, so white, so beautiful.

And they were so very alone.

And from the pool, it was just a few steps back to the warmth of the fire. They would snuggle up in front of it with a comforter, a few throw pillows and a bottle of wine.

They were lying there one night when Justin nuzzled her ear and murmured softly, "I don't want the snow to end. I want it to fall forever."

Kristin rolled to her back and looked up at him. "Ah, but all of your batteries will eventually die. We'll run out of gas for cooking and heat. It has to end sometime."

"And what will happen when it ends, Ms. Kennedy?" he asked her.

She smiled. "Well, I suppose I do need to show up at Roger's for dinner. But you can come with me."

"Thanks. And am I supposed to pretend that nothing happened between us? Pass the peas, please, what is your name? Kristin, oh, yes."

She giggled. "Don't be ridiculous. I'd never ask you to dinner if you didn't know my name."

"Ah, but how does Roger feel about your romantic life?"

"He's my cousin, not my father."

"But?"

Kristin sighed, wondering how he had heard the note of concern in her voice. "All right, so he thinks he's my big brother. We'll go gently with him."

"What if he pulls out a shotgun?" Justin teased lazily. His eyes were half-closed and he watched her like a cat.

"A shotgun?"

"Umm. And demands that I do right by you?"

"I don't think he'd be quite that dramatic. He probably doesn't even own a shotgun."

Justin rolled over, bringing her beneath him. "Seriously. What happens when you leave here? Where do you go?"

"Well, Roger is—"

"I mean after that. Where do you live, what do you do? I'm an open book, you've all of me, and I still don't know anything about you except that you're Roger's cousin. Where do you live?"

"Boston."

"Right in the city?"

"Right in the city."

"Do you work there?"

She nodded, feeling her heart begin to pound and her breath to quicken. Now was her chance. It was the perfect opening. She had to tell him what she did for a living.

"Would you think of leaving the city?" he asked her softly.

She nodded, winding her arms around his neck.

Tell him!

She couldn't do so because a sweet thrill was warming her from head to toe. He was asking her about a future. Just as if he was falling in love with her.

She didn't want to speak to him. To explain.

"You like the country here?" he asked.

"Very much."

"I'm so, so glad."

And she didn't say a word.

She pressed her lips against his and then teased them with the tip of her tongue. A log fell in the fire and the blaze roared up high beside them. His kiss deepened. Her robe parted. His kiss moved slowly down her throat, between her breasts and beyond. Her breath caught, and her mind spun.

And she never told him....

Not then, not later. Not when they stood in the kitchen and she searched through the cans, found some olives and opened the can to pop one into his mouth. She started to turn, but he pulled her into his arms, and his fingers moved in a tender and passionate motion through her hair. "I really think that I love you, Kristin. I love being with you. I love trusting you. In my whole life, I've never met anyone like you. Everyone else has always been out for themselves alone. You're very, very special."

Don't trust me! she wanted to cry out then, but her face was pressed against his chest. The words came to her lips, but they died away.

"I was so certain that you couldn't be real," he murmured. "That you had only come for that story. And I was even afraid that you'd made love for that story."

She felt that she was choking. She was going to tell him. She just had to find the right time to explain things to him.

Before the fire. After they had eaten.

But when they had eaten, they watched the weather report on the little battery-operated television. And then another classic movie came on, and Kristin fell asleep in Justin's arms without ever having said anything.

And she awoke aroused. Awoke with the heated moisture of his kiss moving down the length of her. She whispered his name, and his fingers curled around hers, but his body moved, rubbing erotically against her own as he edged himself downward and downward. And his kiss teased the inner flesh of her thigh, and then the tip of his tongue moved slowly, erotically, more intimately against her and she forgot everything, forgot the entire world and felt an explosion of sensation with just that first touch....

It seemed forever before she could think again. When he left her, she was so sated and exhausted that she fell asleep again. When she opened her eyes, it was morning, and Justin had risen and dressed already. He walked over to her, grinning, producing her jacket, boots and clothing, dried at long last, and announcing that there was almost something like sun out, and that he'd gotten the front door open and there was a winter wonderland beyond it.

The snow had been falling for five days. Inches and inches of it. But now, Kristin discovered, the snow was down to just a few halfhearted spatterings.

Stepping out onto the porch, Kristin breathed in the icy-cold air. It was almost painfully crisp and clean.

Justin set his hands upon her shoulders. "Isn't it beautiful?"

The world was indeed beautiful. Blanketed in white. The sky had lost its angry gray cast at long last, and light, lush shades of blue were beginning to streak across it. The rolling landscape was encompassed in the white snow. The road was gone completely beneath it. Hedges, trees, shrubs, all wore that cloak of glistening white.

"Let's see if we can find your car," Justin suggested.

Kristin agreed, taking a step forward. She laughed as she stepped knee-high in the snow, and staggered forward, nearly losing her balance.

Justin caught her before she could fall. She spun in his arms, laughing. "This is deep snow, all right."

"Oh, it's not so bad," he told her. Taking her hand, he started out. Once she was moving, Kristin discovered that it really wasn't bad.

She let go of his hand, and he proceeded on. She thought that she was moving well, but then she plummeted forward.

Snow covered her lips, her nose, her forehead and her hair. Justin turned back, looked down at her and started laughing.

"That's not nice!" she informed him, struggling up to a squatting position.

"It's just that—you look like an icicle," he told her apologetically.

There seemed nothing else to do. Kristin wound her gloved fingers around a clump of snow.

It was a big snowball. Nice and wet and loose. She stood up and threw it. It fell against his face with the precision of a major league pitch. Kristin gasped, amazed at her own aim.

"You want to play it out tough, huh?" he responded, wiping the snow from his face. He bent down in the white fluff. Kristin turned to put some distance between them.

His first ball sailed harmlessly past her. She stooped to collect another handful, whirled around to throw it. He was almost on top of her. She threw her snowball. He ducked, avoided it and grinned smugly. He started toward her. A little yelp escaped her and she went running forward into the snow.

His snowball landed smack on the back of her head. She laughed, stopped for another and spun around. He was right on top of her this time, blue eyes glistening and primed for battle.

"No, Justin, no!" she begged, stepping backward.

She stooped into the snow herself, watching him warily, her fingers closing over a handful. She tried to hurl the new missile at him, but he suddenly pounced upon her and she shrieked as they both fell into the snow and went rolling in it. She landed upon her back with him straddling her hips, his snowball still in his hands. He grinned wickedly, looking from the huge snowball to her face.

"Don't you dare!" she warned him.

"Challenging me?" he taunted.

She lifted her nose to him.

"You should really be nice," he warned.

"All right—please, don't you dare!"

He grinned and took a little pinch from the snowball and sprinkled it over her face. She tried to leap from beneath him.

"Be nice, you're at my mercy."

"But I've always been at your mercy," she said sweetly.

"Now that was pretty nicely said. A sweet surrender," he said complacently. Too complacently. He wasn't expecting trouble. She caught his hand, trying to send the snowball flying his way.

He wasn't that much off guard. A few flakes hit him, but he turned the tables quickly, and the snowball landed on her face.

She shrieked, protesting, laughing. "I'm freezing!"

"I'll warm you up."

And he could do so, she knew so well. His lips touched hers, and they were fire. Their gloved hands curled together. The snow was soaking them, it lay all about them. It was cold, so cold.

But then there was his kiss. . . .

And then there was a voice, a startling, male voice, calling out from across the snow. "Justin? Justin, is that you? Hey, I don't mean to disturb you or anything, but I've lost a relative."

Kristin could hear a crunch of footsteps coming closer and closer.

Justin had drawn away. He stared down at Kristin. She felt a fierce trembling rake through her as Justin's eyes touched hers. A lopsided smile touched his lips, a smile of regret.

It was over. Their time of being so alone together was over. In a way, paradise was lost. Roger had come.

They had both known that it would end. That the special, exclusive time between them would end.

It wasn't that anything was over between them; they were falling in love, Kristin thought. Justin had to feel the same way she did.

But this particular and very special time was over.

And Kristin just hadn't expected it to end so soon.

"Justin—"

Justin rose, pulling Kristin up with him. "You lost a relative?" he said lightly. "Damned careless of you, Roger. I think I've found her, though."

Roger Doria was bundled into heavy jeans and a leather jacket. He was a few inches taller than Kristin, with the same gray eyes and dark hair. He was lean and handsome, with a fine sense of humor, and he had always been her favorite cousin.

Until now.

He stared at her blankly, then stared at Justin again. Then he frowned. "You're all covered in snow, Kristin. And you, too, Justin."

She would have laughed if Roger hadn't been quite so disturbed.

"We've been having a snowball fight," she told him.

"So I see."

Kristin could tell that while he wasn't sure quite what he saw, he didn't approve one bit. Well, she was certainly over twenty-one, and he was her cousin, not her father.

"How did you find me?" she asked him, wanting to end the uncomfortable silence that had been growing. "And how did you get here?"

"Snowmobile," he said briefly, pointing down the expanse of Justin's lawn to what should have been the road. "Two of the teenagers down the road from me had been out yesterday. They saw the top of your Cherokee."

He was staring at Justin again.

And Justin wasn't about to explain himself. He might know and like Roger, but at the moment, the two men were definitely antagonistic.

Kristin was shivering. She'd gotten soaked playing in the snow, and standing here now, she was very cold. There was no warmth coming her way right then.

"The Cherokee stalled out on me on my way to your house," Kristin said. "Justin helped me out of the blizzard."

"I see," Roger said.

Justin was still silent.

"Can we go in? I'm freezing." Kristin said.

Justin came back to life, but kept a wary eye on Roger. "Sure," he said.

But going in was a mistake, too. They couldn't just stay in the entryway. And Roger seemed to know the house. He walked on into the living room, rubbing his hands together for warmth. He was heading straight toward the fire.

But the comforter and the pillows were still strewn on the floor in front of the fireplace. And an empty bottle of wine was there with their two glasses. And there were towels thrown on the white bricks of the patio floor, just by the door to the pool.

Roger stared from the comforter and the sheets to Kristin.

She shrugged.

Roger glared at Justin. "You seduced my little cousin, Justin!" he said flatly.

"He didn't seduce me!" Kristin protested. "And I'm not your little cousin, I'm an adult."

"She is an adult, and I don't think that I actually seduced her. I was under the impression that it was a mutual thing," Justin said.

Roger looked back and forth between the two of them and shook his head. "Kristin, do you know who he is?" He didn't let Kristin answer that. Red-faced, he turned quickly to Justin. "Lord, I'm sorry, I didn't mean anything by that. I just wanted her to know, can you understand?"

"Sure. I understand," Justin said dryly.

"I know exactly who he is," Kristin told him.

"Well, then . . ." Roger murmured. He sank down to sit on the granite ledge before the fireplace. He looked back to Justin. "Have you got a beer?"

"Yeah, I've a few stuck out in the snow just outside the patio door. They should be nice and cold by now. I'll bring in a few."

"I can go—" Roger began, rising.

"I'll get them," Justin said.

Roger sat down again. He stared across the room at Kristin. "Did you have to get snowbound here?" he demanded as soon as the door had closed on Justin.

"I was lucky I got snowbound here!" she exclaimed softly. "Roger, that storm came so suddenly. If I'd been stuck in my car, I'd be dead by now!"

"I know, I know, we were worried sick," Roger said. "All right, so you were lucky to get stuck here. Did you have to—to get so involved here?"

"I never realized that you knew him before, but from the way he talks about you, I assumed you were his friend!" Kristin said.

"I am. And that's why I never talked about him," Roger told her flatly. "He wanted to be left alone, and I was careful never to mention where his house was. He's had enough media crawling over him for a long enough time."

"Then, if you're his friend—"

"His wife was murdered here, Kristin."

"Not by him."

"How can you be so sure?" Roger demanded.

"Because I really am his friend," Kristin said stubbornly.

Roger stared at her indignantly, then smiled. "I stand corrected. But it happened here, Kristin. And he's a playwright."

"Is there something that I should know about playwrights in general?" Kristin asked him quickly. She could see Justin coming back across the patio.

"No! But he was married to Myra Breckenridge. Probably the most beautiful woman in the world. And theater people live a different kind of life," Roger warned her hastily.

"I hope his life is different!" she told Roger. And he knew exactly what she meant. All those years ago, when she had been determined not to let her parents know just how devastated she was, she had cried on Roger's shoulder and poured out her tales of woe to Sue. "Is he your friend, or isn't he?"

"He's a great guy."

"Well, then?"

"He's my friend! You're getting into much more."

"I know what I'm doing."

Roger couldn't respond. Justin was coming back through the doors that led to the pool, holding three beer bottles.

"Roger." He tossed one over. Roger caught it. Justin looked to Kristin. "Kristin?"

She shook her head. "It's freezing. And you two are drinking cold beer?"

"It does seem like the thing to do at the moment," Justin told her. He stripped off his outdoor coat and cast it over the couch. He was dressed much as he had been that first time she saw him. His shirt today was a blue plaid, his jeans hugged his hips, and his snow boots were high. His hair was still damp, and his blue eyes were cobalt, picking up the dark color of the shirt.

"I'll take her back with me on the snowmobile," Roger said to Justin. "Sue will want to see her."

"I'm sure they'll clear the roads in a few days. Why not wait until then?" Justin said. "I can get her car out of the snowbank, take a look at it, make sure it's running okay."

"But my wife will be worried."

"Not if you tell her that Kristin is all right."

"Wait a minute! Both of you!" Kristin protested. "You're talking about me as if I'm not even here. As if I don't have a say in anything."

They looked at her, surprised. They seemed hurt that she would even protest.

She threw up her hands. "All right, fine. I'm going to make some coffee. And there just might be a gigantic splash of brandy in it, too."

"That sounds pretty good," Justin said.

"Better than beer," Roger agreed.

"Why don't you make three?"

"Sure," Kristin said, adding beneath her breath, "and it's too bad there isn't a football game on!"

Maybe there *was* a football game on. She was glad that she hadn't spoken out loud.

She walked into the kitchen and put the coffee on. While she watched it perk, she felt a cold sensation slowly seeping over her.

They were out there alone together. Roger, who knew her, who knew everything about her life.

And Justin.

Justin . . . who trusted her.

And she had never said anything to him. She had never explained that it was purely happenstance that she was a free-lance reporter herself.

She rushed back to the living room. They hadn't moved. Roger was still seated on the granite ledge, Justin was still standing near the couch. They both looked at her. And smiled.

She breathed a sigh of relief. "The coffee is nearly finished," she said lamely.

Roger nodded. "Great," he said. He sounded nearly cheerful.

Kristin felt better. Then she noticed that Justin was looking as if he could knock down a brick wall.

"But we need to drink it and go," Roger continued. "Sue will be getting worried."

"Roger, you're still forgetting that it's really up to me what I choose to do," Kristin murmured. She looked at Roger, but the urge to stare at Justin again was strong.

"Yes," Roger said, "it is." But there was a reluctant tone to his voice.

Kristin suddenly sensed a stillness in the room. One that was very uncomfortable. One that was made up of tension and slow simmering anger.

Roger didn't notice it.

Justin did.

Justin was creating it.

She exhaled again, then spun around nervously. Justin knew something. And he was doing his best not to explode in front of Roger.

"I'll help you," Justin said.

She stopped, suddenly afraid to be alone with him. "Don't you trust me in the kitchen?" she asked lightly.

Wrong choice of words, she decided. Her heart was hammering hard. He was staring at her as if she had suddenly become his worst enemy.

He strode across the room, pausing as he passed her. His voice was quiet and soft, but lethal.

"I don't trust you anywhere," he said. "Ms. Kennedy."

He started to precede her into the kitchen. She just stood, biting into her lower lip. "If you want to get the coffee by yourself . . ."

Her voice trailed away. He was standing dead still, his back as stiff as a poker. He turned around. He smiled pleasantly at Roger. He took a step back and grabbed her hand. "No, we'll get the coffee together, you sweet little thing you."

He gave her a jerk that nearly catapulted her forward. Roger was staring at them both. She tried to smile at him, too.

Then they were both in the kitchen, and the door was closed behind them. Justin let go of her arm the minute they were there, as if touching her made his flesh burn. And when he looked at her, she wanted to crawl right beneath the island stove.

"Did you get what you wanted, Ms. Kennedy?"

"Look, I really don't know what you're talking about," she began.

"Why, I think you do," he said softly. Too softly. "According to Roger, Lois Lane has nothing on you. Ms. Crack Reporter. Madam Ace!"

"Wait—"

"You're not a reporter?" His ebony brows shot up.

"I am a reporter, but—"

"Oh, God, but I was one hell of a fool, wasn't I?" he said heatedly, his voice rising just slightly. But it wasn't the volume that was rising, she realized. It was the tension in it. The anger. "I really didn't think anyone would take it all quite as far as you did."

She felt her cheeks reddening and her temper flaring. "You stupid bastard!" she said.

He didn't even seem to hear her. "And I fell for it all, hook, line and sinker. This is going to be a dynamite article, I can tell it right now," he said flatly.

"I wasn't writing an article—"

"You just stumbled upon me?"

"Yes!"

"And you had all this time to tell me what you did for a living and somehow it just slipped your mind."

"If you'd just trust me—"

"Lady, I wouldn't trust you for a glass of water if I was dying of thirst!"

It was the end, the absolute last straw. She had known that he might be angry. That was why she had waited so long to tell him. But she had meant to tell him. She had really meant to do so.

And she had trusted him when he casually tossed the word *murder* her way. Maybe it was expecting too much, but she wanted something in return.

"Excuse me," she said coolly, starting by him.

She didn't make it. His fingers closed around her upper arm. When she met his eyes, they were glacial. "Excuse you?" he asked softly. "Good old Roger has come by, and it's time to go. Might as well. You've gotten everything you came for, right? Is that it?"

She felt as if she were choking. The air between them was heavy with tension and anger. His fingers tightened on her arm.

"Let me go."

"Let you go? I tried so hard to do that."

"Don't!" she cried, anguished by the distance and the mockery in his voice. "My God, after everything, this is all that you can see? You told me—"

"I told you what?" he demanded harshly.

"You said things as if you cared, really cared—"

"Oh, and you must have really enjoyed that. Well, you've got your assets and you know how to use them." He closed his eyes for a moment, gritting his teeth and leaning back. And then his eyes were blazing into hers again with blue flames lighting them like a fever. "And Roger asked me if I'd seduced you!"

She tried to wrench her arm out of his grasp. His hold was tight, and he yanked her closer to him.

"You are good," he said huskily. "I mean you are really damned good. You waltz in here with your little act, passing out on my doorstep. And you're all wide eyes and innocence until you've wedged your way in. But to really get at the heart of things, to dig into the core, you've got to get close. Reporters! Damn! They'll really do anything, and you seem to take the prize. There's nothing like sleeping with a man to get at the heart of him, is there?"

She had a free hand and she used it, cracking her palm with vehemence across his cheek. She moved so quickly that he didn't have a chance to stop her.

The slap was loud in the stillness of the kitchen. Then she could see the marks of her fingers forming on his flesh.

He touched his face, his eyes glimmering. She gritted her teeth as his hand tightened on her arm and a rush of violence seemed to tremble through him. For a moment she thought he would strike her back.

Then he released her, his hand falling to his side.

"Go on, then, Ms. Kennedy. Please don't be offended if I don't read what you write."

"I don't intend to write about you, Mr. Magnasun," she said icily. "I find articles about boorish egomaniacal playwrights to be extremely boring!"

She whirled around, heading out of the kitchen. Her hair flew with her and struck her eyes, bringing the tears that hovered near her lashes very close to falling. Blinded, she tried to keep going.

But he caught her again. Caught her and swung her back into his arms.

"Damn you!" she said, pounding her fists against his chest. But the distance between them was disappearing, and she was crushed against him. She tried to twist from the fall of his lips, but they captured and held her own. Hot, searing hot. Filled with all the passion of his anger. The heat filled and warmed her. The passion touched and taunted and demanded a response. She tried to push away from him. And she tried to fight his kiss....

But his mouth was firmly molded over hers. And her lips were parting beneath it. The sweet damp fever of his mouth ignited a searing response within her, and the pressure of her fingers against his chest grew weak. He kissed her and kissed her, his fingers threading through her hair, massaging her nape. Then his hand cupped her cheek and held her still to the leisure of his kiss. His lips parted from hers, touched them again.

And then he spoke just above her mouth, a whisper so soft that it took several seconds for his words to penetrate her mind.

"You really are good. So damned good. It's even hard to let you go when I know the truth about you."

She wondered if there had ever been a whisper more filled with mockery and vehemence.

"And just what is that truth?" she demanded, once again struggling furiously. "I've told you—I'm not writing any article on you!"

"Why not? You've paid the price." His eyes suddenly raked over her. "Maybe you were even worth it. Hell, somebody's going to write that story."

She shoved against him fiercely. This time he was ready to let her go. She didn't know how furious she was until her hand started to fly again of its own volition.

He caught it that time. "Once is enough, I think, Ms. Kennedy. I think you've done your damage here."

She stared at his fingers where they curled around her wrist. "Then get your hands off me, Mr. Magnasun," she said softly.

He opened his fingers, letting her go. She walked to the doorway and then spun around. "I wasn't writing an article on you, Justin. I didn't tell you I'm a reporter because I couldn't seem to find the right time. I didn't want to spoil anything. You see, I really was falling in love with you."

He started to walk toward her.

"But you, sir, well, you just ruined the best thing you ever had!" she promised him sweetly. "And don't ask me to forgive you—"

"That was the farthest thing from my mind," he assured her with swiftly narrowing eyes.

"Because I won't!" she finished, undaunted. "If you dragged yourself five miles through the snow, I wouldn't forgive you!"

With that she spun around. In the hallway, she crashed into Roger, who had been coming to the kitchen to find out what was taking them so long.

"Kristin, where are you going?"

"Out!"

By then, Justin had appeared behind her, his eyes ablaze and his features tense.

"Kristin—"

"I don't want to talk to you!" she announced in a rage. She was going to start to cry if she didn't leave soon. "I don't want to see you again, ever. I don't even want to see a Jon Mountjoy play again as long as I live!"

"But that won't stop you from writing about Jon Mountjoy, will it?" he thundered back.

"Well," Roger said softly between them, "I guess this means coffee is off?"

They both stared at him. He smiled weakly.

Kristin slammed her way out of the house. In a few seconds, Roger followed.

She ran through the deep snow, falling, rolling, until she reached his snowmobile. Roger was with her in just a few seconds, trying to dust the snow from her clothing. He brushed a flake from her nose. "Kristin—"

"Let's just go, Roger, please?"

He sighed softly. "Yes, we'll go," he told her. "But Justin—"

"Don't! Don't even say his name!" she pleaded.

"Kristin—"

"I want to go!"

"All right. It's all right. We'll go."

She crawled onto the rear of the snowmobile. Roger revved the engine to life.

She hadn't cried. Not once. Not even when the tears had stung like crazy at the back of her eyelids.

But as the snowmobile came to life and then shot across the white expanses, her tears fell against her cheeks.

Icy tears, they seemed to freeze there. Searing hot, and bitterly cold.

Like a touch of snowfire.

Chapter 7

"I always liked Justin," Sue said, stirring her coffee absently. It was early the next morning, and Kristin had breakfast on the gas stove for the three of them.

She'd never meant to talk about Justin at all. But by last night, with Sue's sympathetic ear at her disposal, she'd explained a little of what had happened. And Sue listened, wide-eyed and intrigued. She was a pretty woman with soft brown eyes and a wealth of light reddish-brown hair, and she and Roger had been in love forever, it seemed. They had been high school sweethearts, graduating the year before Kristin did. All three were close in age and had gone through all sorts of things together.

If she'd wanted to stay absolutely silent about Justin Magnasun, she'd never have been able to, Kristin thought. Because Roger knew where she had been—and what she had been doing—and he didn't keep secrets from Sue. And Sue had known her for so very long, and acted often enough like a sister. She'd just never have gotten away with saying nothing.

"I just can't imagine him being so cruel to you," Sue finished lamely. "Then again, there are those who would consider you lucky to have left his house alive."

Actually, Kristin wanted to think about something else. Anything else. She'd been furious with herself for crying on the way to Roger and Sue's, and she was determined never to cry over him again. She wanted to think about the traffic in Boston, about work, lunch next week at the Italian restaurant by the Aquarium with the race car driver, dinner with women from a coalition of mothers who opposed drunk driving. Life was going to go on. She could even go out with the young attorney her father introduced her to two weeks ago. He had seemed attractive enough at the time, tall and lean with a tan from a salon, a nice build from his hours at the sports club and warm hazel eyes.

It was just that he paled so next to Justin Magnasun. Paled to insignificance. But anyone did.

The attorney was probably a nice man, and she might have enjoyed herself on a date with him, and she might have dated him again.

But now she couldn't go out with anyone; she couldn't even begin to fool herself that she could. Not until she got over this.

Because she really had fallen in love with Justin.

Fool, she told herself. She barely knew him.

No, she knew him very well. She knew the way he laughed, and she knew the way his eyes darkened and his lashes lowered when he was wary. She knew his temper, she knew his threats, and she knew that even when he mistrusted her the very most, he had taken care that nothing evil could happen to her. He had never taken advantage of her. She knew the way his arms felt, and she knew his kiss and the way he made love to her.

Perhaps they hadn't been together a full week. The days had been more than a year with someone else. Justin was larger than life, and she might be furious with him, and she might be determined that she never did want to see him again.

But she was still in love with him.

"He didn't murder his wife," Kristin told Sue. "I know he didn't kill her."

"I never thought he did," Sue agreed. "But then..." She shrugged. "I did see them together a few times, and anyone might have murdered her."

Kristin ran her forefinger over the rim of her mug. "You saw them together."

"I'm sorry," Sue said. "I keep forgetting you said you didn't want to talk about him."

"Go ahead, forget it. I want to hear about this," Kristin assured her. "I still can't believe that Justin Magnasun was your neighbor all these years and I never heard about it before!"

Sue shrugged. "Bill Cosby had a house out in Petersham for years, and his neighbors never bothered him. We're New Englanders, famous for protecting our privacy, and we extend that to our celebrities, I suppose. Besides, we were never close friends. Justin wasn't here often enough for that when he was married to Myra. He spent most of his time in New York. But he met Roger at the post office or somewhere, and invited us over for dinner. I remember being so excited, thinking I would meet Myra Breckenridge. What a disappointment!"

"Why?"

"Well, she despised us, and everything small-town. She even hated the house. That beautiful, beautiful house that he'd built." She sighed. "The pool is fabulous." She looked over at Kristin speculatively. "Did you . . . in that wonderful pool?"

"Sue!" Kristin felt her cheeks reddening.

"Oh, how romantic!" Sue sighed. "The absolute fantasy. I always wondered what it would be like, the snow falling outside . . ."

"Sue, you were telling me about Myra Breckenridge."

"Oh, well, what's to tell?" Sue shrugged again. "She was a bitch. The night we were there was a disaster. Justin came in with us, and she was upstairs. She came running down insisting they had to go back to New York immediately. She barely acknowledged us when he introduced us, and when he told her he'd invited us for dinner, she said something like 'How quaint.' We felt like Ma and Pa Kettle."

Kristin leaned across the table watching her and grinned. "So what did Justin do?"

"Oh, he wasn't about to take anything from her. He told her to go right ahead and leave for New York, because if she was rude again, he'd send her packing himself. She shut her mouth and ran back upstairs and we didn't see her again until much later."

"It must have been awfully awkward."

"Oddly enough, it wasn't," Sue told her. "Because Justin was charming. They had a cook there at the time—she came with them from New York, I think— and dinner was wonderful. He selected a great bottle of wine for me, and he and Roger sat there drinking beer like a couple of armchair quarterbacks. I'd never met a more natural man. Smooth. He eased over his wife's behavior with incredible diplomacy."

"When did Myra reappear?"

"Umm, near midnight, just when we were about to leave. And what a difference. She came down in jeans and a T-shirt. I've never seen anyone look quite so beautiful in jeans and a T-shirt. And this time she was nice, but it was all a fake. She apologized to Roger and me, she said she had been filming the week before, and she was exhausted. The funny thing about it was that…"

Sue's voice trailed away. Kristin frowned, watching her. She waited. "What?" she demanded then, anxiously. "What, what, tell me!"

"Oh, well, the funny thing is that I think she did love him in her own way. I think she loved him a lot. But they were separated soon after that. She'd been playing in a plastic world so long that she just didn't know how to cope in the real one, and he wasn't that type. Does that make any sense to you?"

Kristin nodded. "I . . . guess so."

Sue sighed softly again, staring at the stove. "I would have loved him."

"I beg your pardon?" Kristin said.

Sue's eyes shot to hers, riddled with guilt. "Oh, I didn't mean that the way that it sounded. I adore Roger, you know that. I always have, and I always will. But…Justin is intriguing, don't you think? Oh yes, well, obviously you agree. He's got such great eyes. And a fabulous body. What am I telling you? You must know much more about that than I do—"

"Sue!"

"Sorry," Sue grinned. But she couldn't seem to help herself, and leaned across the table. "But I do want to know," she said impishly.

"Well, I want to know what *you* know about the murder," Kristin shot back.

"Oh, that," Sue said. "I imagine you know more about that than I do, too. I heard about it after the fact. We were happy for Justin, of course, because *Snowfire* had just opened, another great play like all his others. Rave reviews. We hadn't seen him in a long, long time. Then we read about the murder in the paper. We heard about it from the sheriff, too. And he seemed unhappy that they'd arrested Justin, because he knew Justin, too. But he and Myra hadn't been getting on, and all the others there said he'd threatened to kill her just that night. Everyone knew she'd been playing around, and while they were separated, she was still his wife. Personally..."

"What?" Kristin said, exasperated. Sue kept coming to the point, and then she'd quit speaking.

"Oh, well, personally... I don't think he was in love with her anymore. I don't think she could have made him jealous enough to want to kill her."

"But if she was so beautiful..."

Sue shook her head. "You may become infatuated with someone because he or she is beautiful. But you can't love them blindly for it. Not forever. Justin needed more from a woman than Myra Breckenridge could give. Maybe she wasn't capable of more. It's hard to say. The whole situation was so sad. Roger and I would have been more than willing to stand as character witnesses for him, but he never asked us and it never became necessary. They simply couldn't convict him on the evidence they had. It was all circumstantial."

"All this was going on in my own cousin's backyard and I didn't even know it," Kristin said.

"You were just divorced at the time and trying to avoid the family," Sue reminded her shrewdly. She shrugged. "And we never mentioned Justin afterward because he came here to get away from the curious. And you were never a rag reporter. You do in-depth things on the environment or orphans or animals. I'd have never thought that you'd want to do anything on Justin Magnasun.''

"It's a pity you can't tell Justin that," Kristin murmured.

"Oh! Well, I'll tell him. I'll be delighted to tell him—" Sue began.

"No! I've nothing at all to say to him anymore. Nothing at all."

"Kristin, if that's just pride—"

"It's not pride. It's survival," Kristin said firmly. "Besides, he had nothing to say to me. And I trusted him, Sue. Even when he announced he had been accused of murder, I trusted him!"

Sue was silent for a minute. "Think of it from his perspective. A reporter has called looking for a good piece of gossip. Then this young attractive woman appears at his door in the snow. She seduces him—"

"I never—"

"Okay, but it sounds better that way," Sue said pragmatically. "She doesn't seduce him, she charms him into seducing her."

"It was a mutual decision over chess," Kristin said primly.

Sue cast her a quick doubting glance and then continued. "Okay, they seduce each other—a mutual decision over chess—and then he finds himself giving her all sorts of information about himself. Then he discovers that she is a reporter. What did you expect from him?"

"I expect," a voice announced from the hallway, "that I should have taught you how to play chess better!"

Kristin swung around.

Roger was leaning against the door frame. "Then this whole thing might have been prevented!"

"How long have you been standing there listening?" Sue demanded.

"The chess part, that's all," Roger said woefully. "Just think, if I had been a better teacher, she could have put him into checkmate and they could have moved on to backgammon or checkers instead of sex."

"Oh, Lord!" Kristin groaned, allowing her forehead to fall against the table. "I swear, if you two don't have a heart soon, I'm going home."

"The roads aren't clear yet," Roger told her, rubbing her nape affectionately. "Hey, kiddo, we're really just trying to make it better, you know," he told her softly.

She lifted her head and smiled. "I know." She sighed, then she sat straighter. "Do you know what?"

"What?" Roger and Sue said in unison.

"I *am* going to do a story on Justin Magnasun."

"Oh, boy, he'll really trust you then," Roger said.

She shook her head. "It doesn't matter now, does it? What matters is that . . ."

"Is that what? What?" Sue demanded.

Kristin grinned ruefully. She was doing it now herself. "Well, the real killer has never been apprehended. Maybe I can find something, some motive, some evidence, against someone else."

"And maybe the killer was just someone out for a walk that night," Roger told her. "They could never tell anything from the footprints—there were far too many all over the estate."

"Roger, do you really believe that a killer just stumbled through a town this small to murder a woman at a remote estate?" Kristin asked him.

"No, I don't. But it isn't impossible."

"But it's far more probable that it was someone there. A motive, Roger, that's what we need."

"That leads you right back to Justin."

"That's because the entire thing hasn't been properly investigated," Kristin told him. She could feel the excitement for the task ahead sweeping through her.

She had, of course, told Justin that she never wanted to see him again. She'd been absolutely furious with him. She was still absolutely furious with him.

She did owe him. He had saved her life. If she had stayed in her car, she'd have frozen to death. Even if he had been an unwilling host, he hadn't let her die.

For that, she would prove him innocent.

No matter what it would seem to prove to him about her.

She knew she was still in love with him. Not even the depths of her hurt and anger could take away the strength of that emotion.

The three of them suddenly started as a loud whirring sound was heard from outside.

"Snowplows," Sue said briefly. "The roads will be cleared soon enough now."

"We can go see about your car."

"Oh," Kristin said stiffly. Her car was too close to Justin Magnasun's house. "Roger, couldn't you just—"

"No, you can come with me," he said.

"You're cruel."

"I am not. I can't drive two cars back to the house." He smiled, and left the room.

"Sue—" Kristin began.

Her cousin-in-law shook her head. "I think you should go, too, Kristin. I mean, you're not afraid of him, are you? At this point?"

There was an innocent innuendo there. "I'm not afraid of him," Kristin said.

Sue stretched out a hand across the table, covering Kristin's fingers. "Kristin, I think this is madness. Don't go investigating this case. For one, you could get hurt. The real killer can't possibly want to get caught, and someone who has killed once might find it very easy to do so again. And there is still the matter of you and Justin—"

"No," she said softly. "Sue, he said horrible things to me. Really horrible things."

"Well, Roger has said a few to me, too. And I'm certain that I've done the same to him. But I love him, and I know that he loves me, and we kiss and make up and get by those things. Take a chance, Kristin! You've never trusted anyone, not since your marriage. And you had something there. Something that must have mattered very much."

"I can't forgive him. And he doesn't even want to be forgiven. He certainly hasn't made any attempt to come after me."

"What do you want? The white knight to come and sweep you up on a white charger?"

"Yes, maybe. I don't know. Oh, Sue, I don't really want anything at all. I just want him to come and tell me that the days we had together really meant what we said they did. I want him to know that I didn't come there to use him in any way because he knows me—and knows I wouldn't do something like that!"

"Maybe he does—"

Kristin shook her head firmly. "No."

Sue sighed. "Well, you're going to need your car. To investigate him."

"You won't go for me?"

"You're really not afraid of him?"

"Oh!" Kristin threw up her hands in exasperation. "What if I said I *was* afraid of him?"

"I'd tell you not to be," Sue said complacently. She was standing and picking up the few breakfast dishes that remained on the table. She set a plate in the sink. "At least, I'm almost positive that you shouldn't be."

"That's like Roger. He thinks Justin isn't a murderer."

"Well? We're behind him."

"No," Kristin said softly. "I *know* he's not a murderer. There's a big difference."

Sue smiled, her eyes lowered. "Then you definitely aren't afraid of him. So go change that bathrobe and go and get your car."

"Can I borrow something else to wear?" Kristin asked her, staring down at the soft pink fluffy robe of Sue's that she had already borrowed.

"Make yourself at home. My closet is yours," Sue said.

And Kristin gave up on being reprieved and went to get dressed.

As it happened, though, the plows didn't finish the job that day, and it was the next morning before Kristin and Roger could venture out to try to retrieve the Cherokee from the snowbank.

As they neared Justin's property, Kristin studied the lovely, clean lines of the house. She had never really looked at it from the outside before. She could see the glass windows of the breakfast room off the kitchen and she bit her lower lip, remembering how she had sat in a window seat with Justin, watching the snow fall. The room had been so warm. And the kitchen had seemed as if it had been created for her, with her love of cooking and gadgets. She'd been wonderfully comfortable there.

Though Justin had never explained it, she thought she understood now. The house had originally been a dream for him. A place to go with someone he loved. To share long winter nights. Maybe to learn to cook together. To make delicious dinners and sip hot coffees.

Myra had just had different dreams.

But to Kristin, the house had been perfect. She had loved it, every inch of it. She'd been so comfortable.

So at home.

With his house . . .

With him.

She gritted her teeth and looked away from the house just as Roger began to slow his Blazer.

She thought back to the day when she had arrived here. The car had stalled first at the end of the driveway leading to the house. She thought she had driven quite a distance after that. It had certainly felt like it when she had been trudging back on foot. But she hadn't really. Not at all. She had merely made it around a curve where the road skirted the hill on which the house sat. A few hundred yards perhaps. And the house, the big beautiful house, was clearly visible, sitting up on the hill. In the daylight, the property was even lovelier than she had remembered it.

The snowbank around her car had been partially cleared, as if some kindly state employee had seen her plight and done his polite best to help her out. She made a mental note to write a letter of thanks to the proper department to see that credit went where credit was due.

But there was only so much that a snowplow could do to help. The nose of the Cherokee was still pointed into a huge pile of snow. The front wheels were caught in it, but the back of the vehicle was clear. She could see all her belongings piled up in the back, her suitcases and overnight bag, her little laptop computer and her small dot matrix printer. One of the suitcases had popped open and some of her clothing was floating on top of the bags. It was the wrong suitcase. Soft frothy underwear and a pastel nightgown seemed incongruous spilled out there, so close to the snow.

"You still pack well, I see," Roger told her.

"Oh, will you shut up!" Kristin begged him.

He shrugged. "Well, I'll attach a chain and see if the Blazer can drag her out," he said.

"What do I do to help you?"

"Leave me alone, for the moment, I think," he told her pleasantly.

She made a face at him and leaned against the side of her car, staring out at the forest of trees on the other side of the road. She hugged her arms around herself, shivering. The snow had stopped, but it was bitterly cold outside. There were icicles hanging from many of the trees. The sun, however, was trying to appear. The sky was both blue and gray, still a winter sky. The ice and snow was still spotlessly clean, though. The picture was beautiful, a fairy-tale land, encompassed in a glasslike splendor.

And this was Justin's world....

It was also where Myra Breckenridge had died. She had hated it here, hated the wintry beauty.

He hadn't done it, she was certain. Then she was angry with herself for being so determined he was innocent.

He wasn't determined as she was.

But being here...

She closed her eyes for a minute, trying to imagine the party. It had been winter. Winter, like this. Snow would have lain on the ground, thick. The air would have been cold. Myra was still in love with Justin, but he was no longer in love with her. He had written a play for her, though, a starring vehicle for her. And the major actors had been gathered, a cast of beautiful people, people who were bigger than life. Then there were the agents, Justin's and Myra's. All gathered at the house, with the play a huge success.

Who could possibly have wanted Myra dead? Had it been a crime of passion, or had someone planned it out carefully? What had the conversations been about that night? And what had been the undercurrents within the house?

What an interesting gathering it must have been. Myra, so very beautiful, so highly adulated, but perhaps feeling the strain of the passing years beneath her veneer of casual confidence and command. And the other woman...what had she been like? Roxanne Baynes, the ingenue in the play, young, just beginning. She wouldn't have had a chance to grow so jaded.

Had she been a threat to Myra?

Myra was the one dead, Kristin reminded herself. Not the lovely young ingenue. Time to try again.

What about the men? The handsome leading man, Jack Jones. Perhaps he had been in love with Myra. Secretly. Perhaps she had made him terribly jealous.

What of the critic? Maybe he had been blackmailing Myra....

It seemed hopeless. She didn't know any of them, and she couldn't just imagine a motive for murder.

But what about the critic's wife?

She started suddenly, violently, hearing a voice.

"You want the hooks down on the bumper like that?"

She pushed away from the car, suddenly wary, and taken by surprise.

It was Justin's voice she heard.

She stared at him with a certain panic as he came crunching across the road with Roger's towline. He was wearing a ski jacket and his shoulders looked huge, making him seem even taller than he already was. He was hatless, and his dark hair had fallen free over his forehead. His eyes were a brilliant blue near the dark hair and his ruddy cheeks. She felt her stomach and heart lurch as one, and she gritted her teeth, fighting a wave of emotion that took her entirely off guard.

She wanted to hate him. She wanted to hate him so fiercely. She wanted to keep her anger alive, because it mattered so much that he believe in her.

It hadn't been a full two days since she had seen him. It hadn't been a full eight days since she had met him.

But in that time, he had become her life....

He paused, meeting her eyes. "Good morning, Ms. Kennedy," he said. His voice was husky, soft. It sent sensations sweeping down the length of her spine. And she waited....

Chapter 8

She waited for nothing.

Justin passed her by without blinking an eye. He walked on, ignoring her. He squatted down in back of the Cherokee to attach the hooks of the towline to her bumper. When he disappeared from her view there, she felt a flood of unreasoning fury rip through her. She hurried to the rear of the car.

"I don't need your help!"

He glanced up at her, a dark brow raised. "I wasn't helping you. I was helping Roger."

"I don't want you touching my car!"

"I don't want your car in front of my house."

He finished with the hooks and rose. His eyes fell on her things in the back of the Cherokee.

"Clothing," he commented idly. His eyes met hers. "How nice. You did intend to wear some."

"You'll certainly never see me without them again," she returned sweetly.

"Ah, but certain things will live on in memory," he said lightly. Before she could think of a suitable rebuttal, he was commenting on the contents of the Cherokee again. "And my, my, what else? Could that be a computer? And a printer. What a way to visit relatives. Bring your work right along with you—or acquire it on the way."

"What a talent you have with words," she said. "It's easy to understand why you're a successful playwright—and such an unsuccessful husband."

He stiffened at that, and his smile hardened even more. "I can't wait to read this article. It's easy to understand that you must be a very successful rag writer."

She kept her smile sweetly in place despite the storm raging inside her. "I've never written for any rag papers, Mr. Magnasun. I don't write stories about people like you."

"That's good to hear," he said. His eyes were still fixed on her, but Roger was calling to him, and he turned around to head toward the Blazer. "Nice assortment," he told her, gazing back at the lingerie spread across the back of the Cherokee. "I'd use that mauve piece on your next victim. It's a winner."

In all her life she'd never felt anger sear through her so swiftly. She bent down and found a hard wad of snow and threw it for all she was worth. Just when it cracked against the back of his head, she remembered regretfully that this was exactly what they had been doing when they last parted.

Except this was different now.

This was war.

Justin stiffened, then turned slowly.

And despite Roger, despite her car, despite everything, Kristin decided it might be prudent to run.

Definitely...

Especially when he turned slowly and she saw his eyes. She ran.

In seconds he was after her across the snow. She heard his footsteps right behind her. She tried to veer into the trees but knew she'd never make it. Her flight brought her closer and closer to the house. He was on her heels as she reached the front door. She managed to get inside it, and had almost slammed the door when his shoulders heaved against it, nearly sending her flying. She pushed back against it with all her might.

"What the hell do you think you're doing?" he called.

"Locking you out!"

"It's my house!"

"But you're going to..."

The words died away on her lips. Kill me. They held a different meaning here, and she couldn't voice them.

"You're going to do...something to me," she responded.

"I'd like to do something to you, all right," he muttered darkly. "Open the door! It's my house."

"Promise you're not going to—"

"To what?"

"Throw a snowball back at me."

"I promise I'm not going to throw a snowball back at you. Open the door!"

But he didn't wait for her to open it. He shoved his shoulder against it hard, and it burst open. In a second he had her by the arm and was dragging her back into the snow.

"You promised!" she reminded him.

"That hurt like hell!" he stormed.

"I didn't mean to—"

"Oh, it hit me dead in the center of the neck because you didn't mean to throw it?"

"No...I..." She backed away from him. He made a flying leap at her as a tackle might, and she was flat on her back in the snow and he was straddling her.

"You promised—"

"I said I wouldn't throw a snowball at you. This one is just going to drop down on your nose by accident!"

"But you deserved it!"

He had deserved it. And she hadn't deserved this. His face so close, his hands upon her. His hips locked to hers while his thighs closed around her, hot, tight. Her breathing was coming impossibly fast, and her heart was beating like wildfire. She moistened her lips against the sudden dryness that seized them, and then she felt the touch of his eyes, watching her mouth. And she thought that he wanted to kiss her, and she wanted to feel that kiss so very badly. There was warmth within him, so much warmth, sweet and combustible.

"I *deserved* it!" he grated. He didn't drop a snowball on her. His gloved fingers curled around hers as he held her down in the snow. He leaned impossibly close. His lips almost touched hers. His breath fanned her cheek and she strained against him, only to feel more of his body despite the masses of clothing that covered them both. She could feel so much....

And she could feel that he wanted her then, as much as she wanted him. No matter what their words. Tension rose. They were both trying to speak. Words were lost.

"What, Ms. Kennedy? Are you missing something that you need for your story?" he asked her huskily.

"I could write what a bastard you are already!" she snapped back. God, make it matter! she prayed suddenly. Don't let me forget what he's saying in all this longing....

"Your computer is right in the car!" he challenged her.

"And your life is public record!" she reminded him passionately. Oh, God, his mouth was so close, so very close.

"You want more than public record, don't you?"

So much more, she could have said. But he'd never have understood.

"Get off me, please."

"But I'm talking to you."

"I told you that I never wanted to talk to you again—that even if you dragged yourself through five miles of snow I'd never forgive you. Remember?"

"There isn't a snowball's chance in hell of that ever happening, Ms. Kennedy."

"Then get your two-ton body off mine, please!"

But he wasn't moving, he was watching her. Watching her eyes, his fingers closing more tightly around hers. He was going to kiss her. And she longed to feel his mouth again. The warmth and the searing liquid pleasure of his kiss...

"Oh, come on, guys, please!"

The mournful request came from over their heads. Roger was there.

"Justin, she is my cousin. If you two are going to get into this thing hot and heavy again, just tell me and I'll go away quietly. But if you're trying to sacrifice her to the snow gods, then I've got to step in here!"

Justin grated his teeth and stood, pulling Kristin up with him. They just stared at each other heatedly.

"Well," Roger murmured, "if anyone cares, I've gotten the Cherokee started."

"I care!" Kristin said quickly. She stared at Justin a moment longer, then turned and ran down the lawn. She hurried into the Cherokee, then sat at the wheel a moment, her hands shaking. She had been ready to kiss him again.

No, she had been ready to do anything with him again.

And he hadn't apologized; he had accused her all over again.

She revved the Cherokee to life. Roger had backed it well onto the road for her. She touched the gas pedal, and headed for Roger and Sue's.

The next morning, the sky was actually blue. The weather remained cold, but the sky was beautiful and the snow on the ground remained white and beautiful, too. And the power and phones had come back on.

Roger had driven to Athol where he was teaching, and Sue had a doctor's appointment. Kristin was glad, because she didn't feel like a confrontation with either of them when she decided go through the newspaper morgue in their small-town library.

There was a single librarian there, a friendly, elderly lady. Kristin was careful not to say exactly what she was after—news traveled fast in a small town—but when she tried to hedge, the woman discovered what she was after anyway.

"The murder, of course!" the librarian said smugly. "Well, it's all that's ever really happened out here, so it's what people tend to look up. It is fascinating for a small place like this. Such interesting, famous people! He still has a home hereabouts, but then we keep it quiet, we do. Most of the time," she added, realizing that she was talking away. "Well, he seems to be a fine man, he does.

He's always been good to the townsfolk, helping out, and more. He's just plain friendly, no airs about him.

"Now her...well, she was another cup of tea. If he did wring her neck, can't say as how I'd blame him. Maybe he did. Such a good-looking man, but a powerful one, too, you know...?"

"Yes, of course," Kristin murmured.

"They were all in here the day of that party of his, the day she died. If you want the truth of it, I think the agent, that Artie person, was halfway in love with her. She was disgraceful. But then, Mr. Magnasun himself was being so courteous to that young blond thing, Roxanne-whatever-her-name-is. She's going to be in the play when it reopens on Broadway. Did you know that?"

"No, I didn't," Kristin said.

"The play is going to have the exact same cast—except for Myra Breckenridge, of course. Some say she's haunting the rehearsals, though. Anyway, there's speculation about the case all over again. Hasn't hurt Mr. Magnasun's career any, though, I must say. People do just love a good scandal!"

"Yes, I see that they do," Kristin said.

Since the librarian knew what she was doing, Kristin went ahead and asked her for the exact files she wanted. The friendly librarian set her up with the microfiche and a viewer and then left her alone.

It was just a two-room library, built in the late 1700s and not changed much since then. The librarian was out in the main room with all the books, and Kristin was back in the smaller research room. It was pleasant and homey. She was working at one of several old desks, and there were big leather chairs set before a fire. But there was no one there to enjoy them. Other than herself and the librarian, she had the place to herself.

After a few minutes, even the librarian left. She came to tell Kristin that she was going for some lunch. "I'll be at Tilly's Room and Board place, picking up a sandwich, dear. Can I bring you one?"

"No, thanks, but a cup of tea would be great," Kristin said, reaching for her purse.

"No, no, you're Roger's cousin, and he and Sue are always bringing me goodies. Let me get you a cup of tea."

Kristin thanked her, and the woman left. Small-town life was so very different. The librarian didn't mind a bit leaving the place untended.

Back to work, Kristin told herself. She had found the first of the newspaper accounts.

The world *Snowfire!* blazed across one headline. She scanned the article quickly. It began with the discovery of Myra's body in the snow. It went on to describe the party, Justin's house and Justin's fame. Suspicion was already cast upon him in the article. The names of the other guests were mentioned, but not much information was given about them.

Kristin then found a number of interviews with the guests. The reporter must have loved Roxanne Baynes, the young ingenue, because he gave her a full head shot. There was also a photo of Artie Fein, his head between his knees, weeping.

Kristin drew a pad and paper from her purse and began scribbling out names. Justin had mentioned them before, but she really hadn't paid enough attention.

There were the stars of *Snowfire*—Roxanne, the handsome young Jack Jones and the talented Harry Johnston. There was the film critic, Joseph Banks. Banks...he had commented to the reporter that Myra Breckenridge had chosen to "depart this life just as dramatically as she lived it." Banks's wife, Sara, pictured hanging on to his arm, was wide-eyed, soft, delicate, pretty. Also at the party had been Myra's agent, Artie Fein, and Justin's agent, Christina Anderson, a tall, slinky blonde.

Christina was some agent, Kristin decided. But then she recognized the ugly pangs of jealousy rising in her heart. She had no right to judge Christina Anderson. She'd met several agents in her time, and many of them were bright and attractive young women.

So where did she start? Kristin wondered. Two agents, three surviving cast members, a theater critic and his wife, And the maid, Consuela.

She thought for a minute, and sincerely doubted Consuela would be worth investigating. She had merely been hired for the party, according to the article. There had been no previous connection with either Myra or Justin, and she surely had no reason to strangle Myra. Kristin doubted that Consuela could have hated Myra that much—even if the movie queen had made some disparaging remark about the food or drink for the evening.

No, this was definitely more than burnt rolls!

The single picture of Justin showed him dry-eyed and stoic. He hadn't been going to break. He'd known he was under suspicion, and his defenses were already up.

She tapped her fingers on the desk, then turned back to the information on Roxanne Baynes. Something in one of the articles had drawn her attention. She went back looking for it, wondering what it was.

She scanned the paper and found a mention in one article that Roxanne's hometown was Boston.

They would be in the last few weeks of rehearsals for the revival, Kristin thought quickly. But still . . .

On a hunch she stood up and dug through her purse for her Calling Card. She started to gather up her belongings, but then she shrugged. The librarian had left an entire library of books, a computer and other valuable equipment. Kristin decided to leave behind her things.

She hurried out to the street and looked for a phone booth. There was one just outside the eighteenth-century building at the far side of the town square. She hurried over to it.

After she got through to information in Boston, she thought that she was probably being a fool. She wondered if Roxanne Baynes was even the woman's real name, and she almost hung up before she started. But an operator was already on the other end of the line, and she asked him for a listing for Roxanne Baynes. To her surprise, she was given a number.

She dialed it, and to her further surprise, she reached a recording that gave her a number in New York. Thinking she was on a roll, she dialed again, calling New York City.

She *was* on a roll. A woman with a husky voice answered the phone. A breathy, Marilyn Monroe type of voice, feminine, feline.

"Miss Baynes?"

"Speaking. How may I help you?"

Kristin winced, wondering if she should identify herself as a reporter. She decided to plunge right into the water and see where Roxanne stood.

"My name is Kristin Kennedy, and I'm a free-lance reporter, Miss Baynes. I'm interested in doing a piece on the reopening of *Snowfire*. I was so surprised to hear that the cast was being gathered to perform in it once again."

"Hey, it's a job, and a good one."

"Do you mind speaking with me? I was rather surprised to be able to track you down so easily. I was afraid that you'd be..."

"A little snob with an army of protection?" she asked in the breathy voice. "No," she continued with a sigh. "I'm afraid I'm not a movie star, just a hardworking stage actress. And I don't mind talking about *Snowfire* at all—that is, if you're going to say nice things about me."

Kristin laughed softly. "Well, I don't suppose I'll find it difficult to rave about the play—I understand it's excellent. I would like to find out more about—"

"The murder," Roxanne Baynes interrupted her.

"Yes."

There was a pause.

"Do you think Justin Magnasun was guilty?" Kristin prodded her.

"Who knows? Perhaps she could have died from sheer nastiness alone."

"Was she...mean to you?"

"Myra could be mean to everyone, but she was in seventh heaven when she died. The play was a smashing success and her notices were all raves. I've got to run, Ms. Kennedy, I've got a rehearsal."

"May I call you later?"

"I'll be home in Massachusetts this weekend. Try me then."

"Great!" Kristin said. She thanked the woman, then hung up the phone pensively.

A streak of excitement ran through her. She was on her way to something at last. Smiling, she walked back to the library.

The librarian was still gone, and Kristin's things were right where she had left them. The newspaper microfiche was still in the machine.

Thoughtfully, she looked through more articles. And pictures. There were more of Roxanne, then more of Jack Jones.

Then there was a picture of Myra Breckenridge. Fallen in the snow. Beautiful, silent . . . dead.

Staring at the screen, Kristin realized that a shadow had fallen over it. A large shadow.

And she was alone in the small library.

All alone.

Panic filled her and she spun around and gasped.

A man was standing before the fire. He must have been sitting in one of the chairs there. She hadn't noticed him before now.

But now he had risen. Hands on his hips, he was staring at her. He had been watching her.

Justin.

He walked up behind her and she felt a curious shiver dance down her spine. He was furious, and fighting to contain his fury. His jaw locked hard, he stared down at her with smoldering eyes.

And then he spoke at last.

"So you didn't come for a story?" he demanded harshly. "It doesn't interest you in the least?"

"I—"

"Don't tell me—you just happened to run into these files, right?"

"If you would just—"

"Who were you out calling?" he demanded.

"What?" she cross-queried, wondering just what he knew. How he had found her here?

"Who did you call?"

"It's none of your business!" she snapped. She was shaking. She didn't need to shake, she assured herself. She had a right to do whatever she chose.

But he was standing right there in front of her. Despite herself, she could never forget just how close they had been. Just how his lips had felt against hers, just how provocative his touch could be.

He had a temper like wildfire, she reminded herself. And she was alone with him in this little library. She could see a murderous tic beating against his throat.

He reached down for her, and she swallowed back a scream.

He grabbed her hands and jerked her to her feet. "Just what the hell are you after?" he asked sharply.

"You've no right—"

"I've every right! And I want to know who you were calling out there?"

"Why are you spying on me?"

"Because you're poking your nose into my life, and because I fell for your line once. Once was enough. Now I want to know what the hell is going on."

"Nothing!"

"Let's go," he said suddenly. He pulled her along with such power she couldn't begin to fight him.

"Wait, where—"

He spun back to her with such vehemence that she slammed against him hard. She looked up into his eyes and a flicker of fear did sweep through her, he was so very angry.

"My house."

"No! Wait! I'm not going to your house! You haven't begun to apologize—"

"Apologize!" he roared, looking from her to the microfiche viewer screen where details about Myra's murder blazed away. She reddened.

"You don't understand—"

"I sure as hell do!"

"Oh, you are impossible!"

"Damned right! And I'm going to get a lot more impossible before this is over."

He saw her coat on the rear of her chair and swept it up, then grabbed her purse and thrust it into her hands.

"I'm not—"

"Coming with me? Yes, you are. You want a story, Ms. Kennedy. And I want to know who you called, and just what you think you're going to accomplish. You're going to come with me." He paused, staring at her with his cold blue fury.

"We're both going to get exactly what we want, Kristen. We're both going to get exactly what we want."

Chapter 9

Before Kristin knew it she was bundled back into her coat and headed out to the snow-covered landscape.

"I can't just go with you," she tried to tell Justin. "The librarian is bringing me tea."

"No, Miss Petrie won't be bringing you tea. I saw her on her way over to the inn, and I canceled your order." His hand was on her elbow and he was hurrying her along as he spoke.

She stopped dead still. "You were spying on me!"

They came up to a big white Land Rover. His. He opened the passenger door. "I wasn't spying. I live here, remember? Miss Petrie was kind enough to mention that there was a really beautiful young reporter in the library, dredging up the murder."

"Well, your charming Miss Petrie was certainly glad enough to dredge it all up for me."

"Miss Petrie believes in me. She knows you're Roger's cousin, and she's certain you mean to deal gently with me. I refrained from telling her just how gently you'd already dealt with me."

She wasn't about to set foot inside his car. "And what does that mean?"

"It means you have one hell of a way of charming people. You want a story? Let's go."

"I am not going to your house. And I really have nothing to say to you. I told you—"

"Oh, yes, I'm supposed to crawl five miles through the snow to ask you to forgive me. For being suspicious that you might want to write a story about the murder of Myra Breckenridge."

Kristin sighed slowly. "I didn't come here to do a story on you!"

"But it seemed like such a juicy idea that you couldn't let it go once the idea came up?"

She spun around, ready to leave. His hand landed on her arm, pulling her back. "Who were you calling on the phone?"

"My dear Aunt Lizzie in Tucson," she said sweetly.

His eyes narrowed sharply. "You're going to get hurt, Kristin. You can't play with this."

She didn't know if he was concerned, or still too angry to be concerned. Or if he simply knew something he didn't want her to discover. She looked around the town square. It was beautiful, still whitewashed in snow. The church with its high steeple stood on one side, the city hall on another. The old library was on a third, and the schoolhouse was on the fourth. The inn was just around the corner, and in the center of the square was a snow-covered green with a huge gazebo. In summer there would be fairs here, concerts, games. The scene was very peaceful.

What could happen to anyone here?

Myra Breckenridge had been murdered.

She stared at Justin. His eyes were still piercing into her. Brilliant, bitter.

"I'm not playing with anything," she told him.

"Then what do you think you're doing?" He leaned toward her. "Who did you call?"

"You said you could tell me a worthwhile story for that information!" she challenged him.

He looked so fierce that she almost cringed away from him when he suddenly reached for her and set her firmly into his Land Rover. The door slammed and his feet crunched on the pavement while he walked around the rear of the vehicle.

He crawled into the driver's seat and she looked at him with alarm. "I'm not going to your house—"

"I'll take you to lunch, Ms. Kennedy."

She fell silent as the vehicle jerked and pulled out onto the road. The landscape rolled by them faster and faster as the vehicle picked up speed.

Kristin leaned back against the seat. Justin wasn't in a talkative mood. He turned on the radio, and stared at the road ahead.

Twenty minutes later, he was still driving. He slowed down as they passed through Petersham with its multitude of elegant Victorian houses. It was a magical place, covered with ice and snow. No one stirred on the streets.

"Where are we going?" Kristin persisted.

"Into the town of Barre," he said. Within ten minutes he stopped in another town square beside an old hotel with a huge porch that extended around the corner. Justin walked around and opened the door for her.

She gazed at him. "We're having lunch?"

His lashes didn't flicker. "Did you have something else in mind?"

"Of course not! I was just wondering if we could be civil through a full lunch."

"I can be very civil. I'm just not about to 'crawl' through five miles of snow to beg your forgiveness. Especially since you are writing a story."

"I wasn't—" Kristin began. "Oh, never mind!" she said crossly.

He reached for her hand to help her out of the car. He wasn't wearing gloves, and neither was she. A warmth, electric, shocking, seemed to leap from his hand to hers as he touched her. She met his eyes. So much was still alive and turbulent in them.

"Shall we?" His hand fell to the small of her back. Despite her coat, she could feel his touch. All the way to the bone.

They walked across the street and up the steps to the hotel. In a matter of minutes they were in a warm and elegant dining room with windows that looked out onto the square.

Justin took her coat, seated her and politely asked her consent before ordering a white burgundy. He folded his hands before him, watching her, while they waited for their waitress to bring the wine.

"Civil enough?"

"Very polite."

She looked at him. He was wearing a tweed sweater. It accented the breadth of his shoulders and chest. His hair was crisply dark against it, his cheeks were ruddy from the cold. She bit into her lower lip, resisting the temptation to reach out across the table and touch his fingers with her own.

"It's a pity you can't apologize," she said.

"You owe me the apology."

"I never insinuated horrible things about you."

"I never insinuate anything. I say it outright."

She started to rise.

His hands fell over hers. "Where are you going to go? We're a good half hour from home. You're trapped with me."

"I'm never trapped," she promised him sweetly. Then she broke off and remained seated because their waitress had brought the wine and she didn't feel like creating a scene.

Justin recommended the deep dish turkey pie. She realized she didn't want to leave, but she wanted to order something else just because he had suggested turkey pie. But it really did sound good, and she agreed with his choice. The waitress left them again.

He leaned across the table to her.

"Who were you calling?"

"Maybe it's none of your business. Maybe I have a date this evening."

"Maybe—but you don't."

"And why not?"

He leaned closer. His voice was husky. "Because I don't believe that you could have slept with me the way you did and run out to see someone else."

"Why not? After all, I was only sleeping with you to write a phenomenal story, right?"

"Was I really phenomenal?" he asked her.

She kicked him beneath the table. He laughed, drawing his leg beneath him. She leaned toward him, feeling her temper soar. "You were indeed phenomenal, Mr. Magnasun. Both in rudeness and ego!"

"Kristin—"

"No! Go on, tell me. Why are you so convinced that I don't have a date tonight? I mean, a woman—no, no, a female reporter, like myself—with no morals whatsoever.''

He gritted his teeth, staring at her. "Damn you, Kristin—''

She started to rise again.

His hand fell on hers. "Damn it, will you give me a break? I've been given a pretty rough time by reporters. For the Lord's sake, Kristin, they called me a murderer from the moment the news broke.'' He inhaled sharply. "I'm sorry.''

She took a sip of her wine and felt his fingers curl around hers. A moment ago she would have wrenched her hand away, but now she held still, feeling her heart seem to catapult into her throat.

He leaned toward her, his blue gaze very intense. "Kristin, I don't want you getting involved in this.'' He hesitated a moment. "My agent drove out today. Christina and I have always been good friends, as well as professional associates. I was one of her first clients when she was starting out, and my name helped her pull in more people. Of course the phones have come back on, but she had already started out because she couldn't get hold of me. The media apparently gave the storm a bit of exaggerated coverage, and when she couldn't reach me, she was worried.''

"She was—worried enough about you to drive out here? From New York?" Kristin murmured. She felt the pangs of jealousy tearing at her. "Is she...at your house?"

"No," he answered, seeming distracted as he studied his wineglass. "She's staying at the inn. That's what I was doing in town when I saw your Cherokee at the library and then ran into Miss Petrie.''

Kristin nodded, grateful that at least his agent wasn't at the house. She could remember the picture of Christina Anderson. Tall, attractive, with her sophisticated swing of blond hair. Even her name was attractive.

"Oh?" she murmured.

He nodded, distracted, running a finger over his wineglass.

"How nice."

He looked at her then and grinned slowly. "Jealous? Don't be. She's a friend. She believed in me when no one else did. She was the only one who didn't point a finger at me when the police came. But there's more."

She stiffened, ready for some painful blow.

That was it. He and Christina were platonic friends now, but they hadn't always been so platonic. He'd been having an affair with his agent. Myra had been furious about it. Jealous. So furious that she had . . .

Run out into the snow and strangled herself?

Kristin swallowed hard. Her imagination was running away with her.

"What more?" she asked, trying to sound casual.

"The actress who was playing Myra's part in the re-opening has had to leave the cast. There's a new woman taking the role, Maria Canova."

Kristin lifted her glass, watched him and shrugged.

"Maria is represented by Artie Fein, too. The man who represented Myra. She wanted to meet me, and Christina tells me that Artie is bringing her out over the weekend."

Kristin shrugged again. "So?"

"So, according to Christina, Maria told the rest of the cast that she was coming, and they invited themselves along, too. I don't know when they may be showing up, or anything like that. And I don't like it."

He took a gulp of wine.

Kristin watched him questioningly.

"Maybe I'm overreacting. I don't know. Maybe the cast members won't really show up, after all. Christina didn't seem sure of the details. But one of those people is a murderer. And it's too close to that last party. I don't want you involved."

I am involved! Kristin wanted to shriek. But the waitress had returned with their lunches, and she remained quiet.

She took a bite of her food, and smiled at Justin. "It's delicious."

He groaned. "Did you hear me?"

"Of course, I heard you."

"Who did you call?"

She thought quickly. "I just called the house to see if Sue was back yet. She had a doctor's appointment. She wasn't back yet."

He smiled, leaning back. "Lie again, and I'll never believe a word you say."

He knew she was lying. Rivers of uneasiness swept up and down her spine. She couldn't tell him the truth. He didn't want her involved, and she was involved, whether he liked it or not.

"What difference does it make? You never believed me to begin with. In fact, I really can't believe I'm here with you."

"But you want a good story, right?"

"You haven't given me anything for a good story," she reminded him.

"Okay," he said. He leaned toward her once more. "There was a rumor running rampant that Myra was having an affair with Joseph Banks. That she was so desperate for her career to take flight again that she wasn't going to trust in the play—she wanted to make sure she could get an endorsement from Banks.''

"Really?" Kristin asked.

He nodded. "What else? There was Jack Jones. He was trying to have an affair with Myra, so rumor went, because he thought she could further his career."

"There are motives all over the place!" Kristin exclaimed.

He smiled. "There are rumors all over the place," he corrected her. "Here's another one. Myra hated Roxanne Baynes. Despised her. She called her a cheap little scene stealer. Rumor has it that what Roxanne really stole was one of Myra's lovers."

"Then—"

"Let me see, what can I tell you that isn't rumor? There was one sensational blowup at the party."

"There was?" Excited, Kristin set down her fork. "What happened?"

"The huge blowup between Myra and myself. I told you, I was mad enough to throttle her. And she was dramatic. Everyone heard her say that I'd threatened to kill her, and then, hell, she kicked poor Jugs and I did threaten to kill her. In front of everyone."

Kristin set down her fork and looked across the table at him again. He was studying her intently.

"So then you walked out into the snow," she said.

"You know, by a lot of circumstantial evidence, I do look very guilty."

"Yes, you do."

"Afraid to drive home with me?"

"I was never afraid of you. Except when I thought you were going to shoot me with your shovel," she corrected herself.

He grinned, lowering his head. "Want dessert?"

She shook her head.

"Coffee?"

She shook her head again. He motioned for the check and paid it, then he helped her back into her coat and they left the restaurant.

In the car once again, Kristin mulled over the night of the party in silence for a long while as they drove. Then she realized they were nearing the town square again, and that she might not have a chance to question him again.

That she might not see him again.

"What else was going on that night? You and Myra had a blowup, but what about the others?"

He shrugged. "I really don't remember."

"Try."

"Christina and Artie Fein were discussing the merits of various actors and actresses. Like I said, Joseph Banks and his wife just sat on the sofa by the fire. Myra was flirting—"

"With whom?"

"With anyone. When she wasn't fighting with me, that is."

"And the others?"

"I don't remember."

"You're not concentrating."

His gaze shot quickly to her. "And you haven't told me who you called. And none of it should matter, because you're not writing an article, right?"

"Oh, I do intend to write an article. Eventually. I'm going to expose the truth," Kristin announced.

"A champion for justice?" Justin asked with a laugh.

"I can't believe that you don't care anymore!"

"I do care!" he snapped back.

"Then—"

He pulled the car off to the side of the road and swung around to face her. "Why the hell do you think I allowed the play to open again? Why did I insist upon the same cast? I wanted them thrown together again, I wanted to see if sparks would fly. I just didn't want—"

He broke off, staring at her, then said, "I didn't imagine there would be a nosy little reporter around to get involved."

"I can take care of myself."

He sniffed, a sound that wasn't particularly complimentary. He started to drive again, and she realized that they weren't heading for the town square and her own car at all.

They were heading back to his house.

"Where are we going now?" she asked uneasily.

His eyes met hers in the rearview mirror. "My house."

"I told you—"

"You told me that you wouldn't come here. I told you all sorts of things. And you've yet to tell me who you called."

"I'm not going to tell you—"

"You're staying until you do," he promised her softly.

He meant to carry out his words, she realized quickly as the car turned into the long drive that led to his house. He parked right in front, got out and walked around for her.

She stared at him, seething.

He grinned. "Okay, don't tell me. We can play chess."

"I'll never play chess with you again," Kristin vowed.

He was still grinning. "It's very cold out here."

She swore softly and stepped out of the car. She stared at the house as if it were a living, breathing entity. One that worked Justin's will.

"I'll call Roger."

"Do that. Invite him to dinner. I seem to have a cook in residence once again."

Kristin exhaled on an aggravated note and preceded him up the few steps to the house. He was behind her with his key, and opened the front door for her.

She swept through the entrance and walked to the living room. Despite the warmth in the house she shivered and crossed her arms over her chest. She walked to the rear of the room and stared out at the pool, remembering the way they had been in that pool, then decided that wasn't such a good idea.

"So you really want to write an exposé on the truth," he murmured from behind her.

She spun around. "Yes."

He smiled. There was a tenderness to that smile. "You can still be so convinced that I'm innocent?"

"Yes," she said flatly.

He strode across the floor to her. She felt the warmth of the room sweeping around her. She shouldn't be here. She had been such a fool. She had believed in him, but he would never believe in her.

She should run, she realized. But she was trapped. The doors to the pool were behind, but Justin was between her and escape through the front of the house.

"Justin..." she murmured.

He reached her. He touched her chin, lifting it. His eyes searched hers.

"Don't," she whispered.

"Why?"

"Because I believe in you. And you don't believe in me."

"Convince me," he whispered softly.

No. She started to form the word with her mouth, but the sound never came. His lips covered hers, forming over them, muffling sound, silencing the dictates of all logic. She set a hand upon his shoulders to push him away. She didn't manage to do so. Her fingers curled into his jacket.

He touched her cheek, his hand cupping over it. His tongue flicked over her lips, his kiss seared her throat. She trembled as that kiss traveled to her earlobe, and then back to her throat. Her coat was falling to the floor. Her arms wound around him.

Then she twisted, burying her head against his chest.

"I'd never hurt you," he whispered.

"But you have hurt me. You said horrible things to me."

"I'm sorry," he murmured. "I really am sorry."

She was lifted up into his arms. She stared into his eyes. He returned her gaze, heading for the stairs.

She moistened her lips. "What are we doing?"

"Going upstairs to bed. Unless you'd rather play chess."

She couldn't help but smile. And her eyes fell closed, lazily closed. Despite the ferocity of his temper, this was where she had wanted to be.

The steps disappeared one by one. In seconds she was lying on his bed with its sleek black sheets. Her shoes were falling to the floor, then her sweater, and her jeans. He stripped off his own sweater and crawled down beside her. His lips touched hers, then her chin. Then the pulse at her throat. And his hands were busy, releasing the lacy strap of her bra. His lips fell where the strap had been. Then traveled into the shadowed valley between her breasts.

She inhaled sharply. "You were supposed to have traveled through five miles of snow," she reminded him huskily.

"No," he responded, his mouth against her flesh, "I was supposed to have crawled through five miles of snow."

He rose above her for a moment, a wicked smile in place. "I'll make it up to you, I promise."

Before she knew it, he had turned her onto her stomach. And his whisper touched her lower ear, haunting, damp, sending spirals of sensation to warm her. "I'll crawl my way through five miles of flesh..." he teased.

"Five miles—!" she began to protest, but then a soft "Oh!" escaped her.

He was beginning his journey, sweeping her hair from her neck, his touch, his kiss, landing there. And then the tip of his tongue was on her spine, warm, fascinating, moving downward. Slowly. So very slowly.

All down her back, teasing her until his kiss roused the flesh at the very base of her spine. And then he was kissing the rounded flesh of her hips and her buttocks. She started to twist, but his hands held her there, and he kissed her longer, telling her that he hadn't begun to reach five miles.

But her flesh was afire, and she cried out softly to him, and she was winding her way into his arms. Their lips met again, parted and met. Her fingers raked down his back, stroking, teasing. She pressed her lips against his chest, teasing the hair there with her tongue. Then she found herself pressed back into the endless pillows again, and his mouth was forming over her breast. And his tongue lay against the peak of it, tasting, teasing, moving erotically. He moved down the length of her and she begged him to come to her.

"Five miles..." he whispered.

He found a very erogenous zone at the back of her knee, and one on the side of it. One against her inner

thigh, and one against her upper thigh. Her fingers
wound into the covers in an anguish of expectation. She
wanted him to kiss her there . . . she wanted him to take
her, to end the agony of questing and longing.

"Five miles . . ." he whispered again.

Blinding sensation seized her, and she moved against
him. The sweet, soaring sensation became more than she
could bear. She cried out again, feeling the ecstasy sweep
over her, seep from her. She heard his throaty laughter,
and then he wrapped his arms around her. And she
wanted to whisper that he had gone too far, that she
could take no more. But the words never left her lips,
and he was within her, and to her amazement, all the
sensations were growing again, spiraling again.

And bursting upon them both.

Moments later, he was pulling her against him. His
lips just brushed her forehead.

"I've missed you," he murmured. "I've missed you
more than I thought I could ever miss anyone."

"I've missed you, too," she murmured. She curled
against him, running her fingers over his chest. "You
apologize very well," she told him.

He was silent. She pushed up against him, suddenly
very suspicious.

"You didn't mean a word of it!" she said angrily.

His lashes fell quickly, but she thought she had seen
the truth in his eyes.

"You didn't mean it!" she repeated.

He opened his eyes. Impatient, he tried to pull her
back into his arms. "I did mean it. I'm sorry that I said
horrible things. I know you slept with me only because
you wanted to, because this . . . this is wonderful between us."

"And?" Kristin prompted.

"Isn't that enough?"

"No!" Kristin screamed.

"Then quit lying to me!"

"Lying!" Enflamed, exasperated, Kristin jumped out of bed. She stumbled quickly into her clothes. He watched her for a moment, then rose himself and reached for his jeans. She was already heading for the door when he caught her.

"Kristin—"

"I give up! I never know what you're talking about! Trust is something that matters to both of us. And it's something that I always gave you. I expected so little from you, I asked so little from you. But you couldn't even give me that in return."

"Kristin!" His hands were on her shoulders, holding her there.

"Let me go!"

"Look, I'm trying to give you everything, but you—"

"Trying! Trying isn't good enough! If you have to try, the whole thing is worthless!"

She was going to cry again, she thought. Damn it. She was always leaving this place with tears in her eyes. "Let go of me, Justin."

"Where are you going? I brought you here, remember?"

"But I'm never trapped, do you remember that?"

He exploded with an oath. "I'm not trying to trap you. I want you to go home tonight. You want me to trust you but you never tell me the truth about anything! Just hold on and I'll drive you to your car." He turned around, sat on the foot of his bed and pulled on his socks. Kristin stayed by the door, staring at him numbly.

"What did I lie about?" she asked him.

He pulled his sweater over his head and stared at her. "The phone call!"

She gasped softly. Damn! She'd forgotten all about the phone call. But she still didn't dare tell him the truth.

"I told you—"

"A lie."

"Trust me—"

She could hear his teeth grating together. "Who did you call?"

"What makes you so sure that my phone call had anything to do with you?"

"Oh, just the fact that you were digging through my past life at the time."

"I do have a life of my own, you know."

"Yes, but you seem to be obsessed with mine at the moment."

"I'm not obsessed at the moment at all," she said pleasantly. "Just with leaving. I have to get back to Roger and Sue's."

"We have to talk about this. I want to know who you called."

"I can't talk about anything right now!" Kristin insisted. "I have to go!"

She turned from him quickly and started to walk. She still needed a ride, and he could hound her then, but she wanted to be out of the house.

There seemed to be safety outside. Inside, she was too vulnerable. Intimacy was dangerous.

She passed through the sitting room. When she heard him coming behind her, she hurried down the stairs.

She had just reached the bottom step when she heard the doorbell ringing. She stared at the door. It was his house; she didn't know whether to open the door or not.

He was behind her, wearing his jeans and now his shoes, but still shirtless since he had been coming in pursuit of her. She stood on the bottom step, and he walked past her, glancing her way.

"Who is it?" she asked him tensely.

"I won't know until I answer it," he told her.

Someone connected . . .

Christina Anderson, his agent. Maybe Artie Fein, Myra's agent. Or the new member of the cast, the woman who wanted to meet him, Maria Canova.

She felt her muscles tightening as Justin walked across the entryway to throw open the door. She had the strangest feeling that things would begin to happen. The play was reopening.

"Justin!"

Kristin heard a soft voice, and frowned. Then she smiled slowly. So much for intuition, and things beginning to happen.

"Justin, we're so sorry to bother you. But I can't seem to find Kristin anywhere, and her car is still outside the library. Miss Petrie suggested that she might be with you, since you had come by and spoken with her."

It was Sue.

And Roger was with her. Justin's lip curled slightly as he widened the opening of the door. Kristin could see the two of them standing there on the step together, hand in hand, like a pair of schoolchildren.

And they could see her, too.

"Oh, no," Roger groaned, looking from Justin to Kristin, and then down at Sue. "They've been at it again. Playing chess!"

"Hey, no secrets in this family," Justin said dryly. He gazed over at Kristin. "You told them about chess?"

"Roger!" Kristin grated.

"Well, are you coming in?" Justin asked politely. "It's cold out there."

Roger started to come in; Sue dragged him back to the porch. "We didn't mean to interfere. We were just worried," she said.

"Is it that late?" Kristin asked.

"No, no, we just had an exciting piece of information to share, and—"

Justin reached out for Sue's hand, pulling her into the house. Roger came along with her.

"Well, we didn't want to bother you with personal things, Justin—" Sue began.

"Hell, you know all about chess. I'm anxious to hear about anything personal."

Sue smiled, then she turned to Kristin. "Guess what? You'll never believe it! After all these years. I was so very anxious. I thought I was right, but I didn't know for sure, you know—"

"Sue!" Kristin said.

"We're going to have a baby! Roger and I are going to have a baby!"

"Oh, Sue, how wonderful!" Kristin said. She jumped down the last step and threw her arms around her cousin-in-law enthusiastically.

"Well, this definitely calls for a celebration," Justin said after he had congratulated Roger. "Champagne, the works."

"Where should we go?" Sue asked.

"I know the best place in the world," Justin told her. "Lots of ambience, and the best chef in the area."

"Where's that?" Roger asked.

"Right here. You two sit down and make yourselves comfortable. Madame chef here—" he indicated Kristin "—and I will take care of everything."

He smiled at Kristin, complacent, smug.

She didn't have to go anywhere anymore. He'd have the entire evening to plague any answers from her that he wanted.

Chapter 10

"Roxanne," Justin said suddenly.

Kristin, who had been sprinkling paprika over lobster tails, turned around and looked at him.

Justin was at the island counter, skewering steaks and splashing them liberally with teriyaki sauce. Thanks to the generator on his deep freezer, none of his well-supplied stock of meat and seafood had been damaged by the electrical failure, and they had managed to come up with a menu worthy of the occasion. There would be corn on the cob, broccoli with hollandaise sauce, the lobster tail and the filets.

And Kristin had to hand it to Justin, he did have a sense of the romantic. He seemed genuinely pleased for Roger and Sue, sensing without much of an explanation that the two of them had nearly given up on having children.

The expectant parents were out in the patio area now, sipping champagne—only one glass for Sue, and she'd be sipping it very slowly. A round glass table had already been set for them with a red cloth and snowy napkins, crystal glasses and a three-tiered candle.

There was a pillow beneath Sue's feet, and Justin had managed to find a red flower from one of his house plants, and it lay on the table before Sue.

Now he was being competent in the kitchen, and he hadn't even said a word to Kristin about the stupid phone call.

Until now.

"It was Roxanne," he said flatly. "You called Roxanne."

Kristin turned back to the lobster tails, stubbornly silent.

"Damn it, answer me."

She shrugged. "You seem to know."

"I do."

She swung and smiled at him, leaving her lobster to check the temperature of the oven. She kept her eyes low. He knew. And he knew, of course, that she was actively delving into the murder. She had to make light of it.

"Just think, a good sound guess an hour earlier, and you could have saved yourself this evening."

"I'm enjoying this evening. I like Roger and Sue. And they've been to dinner here before."

"I know," Kristin said. "I heard that Myra wasn't terribly gracious."

"She wasn't. But they've been here since Myra died."

Kristin glanced at him, surprised. He popped an olive into his mouth, and she gazed back at the oven racks. "Sue didn't mention that they'd been here several times."

"It probably slipped her mind. Once you started spilling the details of our sex lives, such trivial things such as dinner were undoubtedly passed on by."

Kristin wrinkled her nose at him. "I didn't spill intimate details about our sex lives. It was really your fault. I mean Roger knew... and I was just trying to explain that it had been a mutual thing."

Justin didn't answer. He just popped another olive into his mouth, watching her with a smug look that made her want to give him a good whack.

She decided to ignore him. "It's nice what you're doing for them anyway. It's better than a restaurant. It's so intimate out there. It means a lot to them. And Sue loves this house. Especially the pool area. She was asking me what it was like—"

She broke off. Sue had been asking her about sex and the pool. A flush covered her cheeks that didn't come from the heat in the kitchen. She quickly tried to think of a way out of her words.

"She asked you about what?" Justin demanded, leaning over the counter to watch her more closely.

"Nothing."

"Oh, no intimate details, huh? You just told her about every room in the house."

"No!" Kristin protested, but he was laughing.

"We should have arranged to leave. That might have been the nicest thing to do for them tonight."

"Well, we can—"

"Not until after we eat," Justin stated. "I want my lobster tail. We'll serve them, we'll socialize, and then we'll slip away, letting them know we'll be out for a long, long time. How's that?"

"Romantic," Kristin told him with a smile. "Thanks. That's really nice."

"Except that you have to stay with me," he warned her.

"Stay with you?"

"Yes. You were trying to walk out on me when Roger and Sue arrived. Remember."

"Yes, I remember," Kristin said, her eyes narrowing. "Because I can have very little to say to you when you don't believe me."

"I didn't say—"

"Yes, you did. And then you lied."

"I never lied."

"You certainly did. You and your five miles of flesh."

"Oh, well, in the heat of the moment . . ."

Kristin shut the oven door on the lobster tails. "You can just take your filets out to the gas grill. And maybe hop on the fire with them."

"Does that mean a movie is off?"

Kristin gritted her teeth. "There isn't a movie anywhere around—"

"Sure there is. We'll drive over to Athol. Truce for the evening?"

She'd forgotten. It was a big, big evening for Roger and Sue.

"Only in honor of my new cousin-to-be," she told him.

"Of course."

Whistling, he turned around with his plate of steaks and went on through to the patio with them.

Within an hour, they had all eaten. They'd discussed names for the new little Doria-to-be, and Justin had made decaffeinated cappuccino for Roger and Sue with rock candy sticks stuck into the mugs.

Then Kristin tried to be casual about saying she and Justin were going to a movie.

"Don't you want us to come with you?" Roger asked.

"No!" Kristin said.

"Oh." He sounded a little hurt. "Well, then, Sue and I will just go home—"

"Oh, you dummy!" Kristin cried. "We're trying to leave you romantically alone!"

"Oh!" Roger seemed to turn a million shades of red. "Oh, that's really nice. But—"

"There are towels in the cabana bath. The door's right over there," Justin told Roger. "In case you two decide to go for a swim. We'll probably take in a show and maybe have coffee somewhere, and then head back. We'll be several hours, I imagine, getting in and out of Athol." He was on his feet, pulling Kristin to hers. "We'll see you in a while, okay?"

Roger stood, his hands in his pockets, his cheeks still a warm shade of red. "Listen, you two, you don't have to do this, we have our own home—"

"But it doesn't have a pool like this!" Sue said, tugging at his hand. "Roger, sit down. Justin?"

"Yes, Sue?"

"Thank you!"

Justin grinned and caught Kristin's hand. "Come on."

Kristin looked back as he led her out. "We'll probably head back to your house first," she told them. "Have a nice evening."

Within a few minutes, they were driving away in Justin's car. Kristin smiled, leaning back in the seat. There was such a nice feeling about having left Roger and Sue there so happy in the middle of a fantasy come true after all their years of marriage. A good marriage. Ten years of it. They'd always stood beside each other, supported each other. And they were still in love.

"Happy?" Justin asked her suddenly.

"Yes. Very."

"They've wanted a child a long time, I take it?"

"Yes. That's the most wonderful thing about them, though. No matter what went wrong, they supported each other instead of casting blame. They never turned to others, they always believed in each other."

"It's what marriage is supposed to be," Justin murmured. "Now there's the fantasy."

Kristin cast a quick glance his way. His eyes were on the road. He must have been thinking about Myra. Kristin leaned back again. Her own marriage had been such a disaster. She was suddenly envying her cousin and Sue with all of her heart. They were already living the fantasy, she thought.

"What do you want to see?" Justin asked her.

"Are we going to have a choice?"

"Probably not."

Kristin grinned, leaned back and closed her eyes again.

And that was a mistake. Within a few minutes she had sunk down in the seat. A few minutes more and her head was falling, and soon she was sound asleep on his lap.

When she woke up, he was smoothing back her hair. "Kristin."

Startled, she struggled up from his lap. "Are we here? The movies?"

He shook his head. His eyes were bright in the moonlight. "I drove to Athol but you were sleeping so soundly that I turned around and drove back. We're at Roger and Sue's."

"Oh! Oh..." Disoriented, Kristin looked around. Roger's front door loomed before her. She looked back to Justin. "You drove all the way to Athol and then all the way back?"

He shrugged. "Sure."

She smiled, lowering her head. "Come on in. I'll try not to be so rude again."

Justin followed her into the house.

It was old, several hundred years old, but very warm with hardwood floors, pleasantly papered walls and comfortable furniture. It was immaculately clean, but with a nice lived-in feeling that instantly made people feel at home.

Justin was no different. While Kristin hung their coats, he moved into the living room, looking at the VCR. "At least we have our choice of movies here. Ah! How about *Lawrence of Arabia?* That will give them several hours!"

Kristin grinned. "Fine."

Neither of them sat on the couch. By some instinct they wound up on the floor together, heads resting on throw pillows, a down comforter pulled over their legs. They watched the movie in silence for a while, and then she felt his chin moving subtly on her head as she was nuzzled back against him.

"What happened after your divorce?" he asked her, and his tone was serious.

Kristin shrugged. "I told you. I went home. I went back to school. And then I worked. Hard."

"Reporting?"

She listened for a barb in his tone. There wasn't one. She turned in his arms, looking into his eyes. "Yes. I started with one of the daily papers, and then I went to one of the newsmagazines."

"No involvements?"

"What?"

"No more involvements. After your husband?"

"Oh." She felt soft color rising to her cheeks. "I was busy."

"I'm glad."

"Why?"

"Because you're very beautiful. And you're fun. And you cook. And you play chess really delightfully. And if someone else had snatched you up..." He shrugged. "Well, we wouldn't be here now."

A searing warmth settled over her. "Ah, yes, but I'm after a story, remember?" she murmured.

"I'm doing my best to give you a good one. Let's see, a newspaper, and then a newsmagazine. And then you went on your own?"

She nodded. "It gave me the freedom to choose what I wanted to write about." She bit her lip, wondering what emotion flicked through his eyes. To choose...and she had chosen him, he must be thinking.

"Justin, I didn't—"

"You know, I was just thinking that you really have had incredible faith in me."

She smiled. "Yes, I have."

"You've never doubted me."

"Never. At first I was certain that you were a maniac," she told him solemnly.

He grinned. "And then . . . ?"

"Then I simply believed."

He watched her for a long time. "Like Roger and Sue. Endless faith. And support."

She didn't say anything. She watched him.

"I believed in it once. And then..." His voice trailed away. He leaned close over her. His lips touched hers, softly, tenderly. "Kristin?"

"Yes?" she said softly.

He started to speak, but a jarring ring suddenly interrupted him. They stared at each other, startled.

"It's the phone!" Kristin said with a laugh.

Justin moved back and Kristin scrambled to her feet. She hurried to the phone on the stand by the sofa.

"Hello?"

To her amazement, it was Sue.

"Thank heavens you're there!" she said. "Roger said you two would never really make it to a movie, that you'd be at our house."

Kristin stared at the receiver for a moment, puzzled. Damn Roger! He knew her too well.

"Kristin?" Sue said anxiously.

"Yes, yes. I'm here. What's the matter?"

Justin was already standing, watching her with a frown.

"This isn't a fantasy, Kristin. This is bedlam. There are people here!"

"What?"

"A woman who says she's Justin's agent arrived, and then right after that, a man showed up with a carload! Seems there is a lady—Maria Canova—taking over a part in Justin's play. And she wanted to meet him. So the cast decided to come here together.

"Kristin—there are six people out in the living room. And my stockings are still draped over the Jacuzzi. Do you think you two could come back?"

Justin was already walking to the stand by the door for their coats. He must have caught some of what Sue was saying.

"Tell her I'll be home right away," he said.

Kristin did so, and hung up quickly. Justin was already striding for the door. "Hey!"

"What?"

"You forgot something."

"What?"

"Me!"

He hesitated. "You're not coming with me, and you're not coming around at all, do you hear me?"

Kristin stopped dead before the kitchen door.

"Justin—"

"Sorry," he said, suddenly harsh. "You're not getting this story."

"I'm not concerned because of a story—"

"And you're not coming!"

"You have to take me back to my car!" Kristin said, amazed. This evening things had been warm, wonderful. She had been certain that he was about to really apologize to her, to tell her that . . .

That he loved her, and that he knew she wouldn't have come to his house simply for a story.

But now, suddenly, she barely knew the man before her with the stubborn twist to his jaw. His eyes were like steel, and his will seemed every bit as strong.

"Justin," she insisted, "you have to take me back to my car!"

He stared at her, turned around and left, letting the door bang shut behind him.

Kristin grabbed her coat and followed him anyway. "Justin!"

He was already in the driver's seat of the Land Rover. He shouted to her. "Get the hell away, Kristin! Do you hear me? No story tonight. No matter how great you are to sleep with!"

Kristin started to run for the car, but the motor was already revving. Before she could reach it, the car was pulling out of the drive.

Tears of frustration stung her eyes.

He didn't mean it. He couldn't mean it. He was just worried about her.

That had to be it, wasn't it?

She didn't know. Agonized, angry, uncertain, she kicked the side of the house. It didn't help any.

And there were no cabs in this neck of the woods, she thought mournfully. It was certainly too far to walk in this weather.

There was only one thing left to do. As soon as Sue and Roger returned, she'd have to take their car.

Angry, anguished, she slowly returned to the house.

It was about an hour before Roger and Sue returned. By then it was well past ten, and Kristin was exhausted, but she had used her time to shower and change and sweep up her hair. She didn't feel like arriving in jeans. In stockings and a soft black dress and heels, she felt a little more up to the arrogance she was going to need to burst her way back into Justin's house when Justin was determined that she wasn't invited.

There was no story tonight…no matter how good she was to sleep with….

She longed to slam her fists against his chest or to strike him, to make him cry out. There was no choice for her but to believe that he didn't mean it. She had to go back. Had to.

When the car turned into the drive, Kristin was ready. But when Roger and Sue walked in, Roger, too, had a stubborn set to his jaw.

"He said you'd try to borrow our car and come over," Roger said.

"What?"

"Kristin, it's late. Go to bed," Sue told her.

"I'm not going to bed, and I need to borrow your car, Roger. Just to go and get my own!"

"Kristin, I can't take you at this time of night!" Roger protested.

Sue looked angry. "You don't want to go over there! He's already flirting with that half-witted blonde. Oh, Kristin, I'm so sorry. I like Justin, I encouraged you! But the way he's acting now...you don't want to go over there!"

"What half-witted blonde?" Kristin asked.

"That Roxanne Baynes. Honestly, she may be a famous actress, but she's a twit. Even Roger says so. How Justin could even consider a flirtation with her after having been with you... Kristin, honestly, I am sorry!"

"Sue, don't worry. You're going to be a mother, remember? You've got to go to bed. But please, let Roger take me for my car. Do you want me to walk?"

"She wouldn't, would she?" Sue asked Roger uneasily.

Roger shrugged. "You've known her as long as I have. She might."

Sue sighed. "Kristin, he'll just humiliate you. He'll leave you standing out in the snow."

"Sue, let me take care of myself this time, okay? He won't leave me in the snow. That much I'm sure of. Roger?"

Roger looked unhappy, but he kissed Sue's cheek and opened the door for Kristin.

Kristin kissed Sue's cheek, too. "I'll be all right."

"I don't know, Kristin. Someone did murder Myra all those years ago—"

"It wasn't Justin," Kristin said certainly. "And I intend to stick to Justin like glue."

"He won't let you—"

"I'm not giving him a choice."

She smiled at Sue with a reckless bravado and prodded Roger out the door. And as soon as they were seated in his Blazer she told him, "I don't want to get my own car. I just want you to let me off. Then he'll be stuck with me."

"Kristin, think about it. What if—" Roger began, his tone anguished.

What if Justin had murdered Myra? She wasn't going to let him say it.

"There is no 'what if,'" she insisted. "He didn't do it, I know it."

Roger clenched his teeth hard. Stubbornly. "I'll take you there. But I'll watch you."

"You can't watch me. I'm going to stay all night."

He exhaled. "Damn it, Kristin, you're almost thirty, and I can't tell you who and who not to have a relationship with. I can't follow you into this man's bedroom. Please, don't—"

"Roger, I'll be all right. Just take me there, please."

He did so, driving in a tense silence. It wasn't far on the cleared roads. When they reached Justin's house, he pulled into the drive. There was a huge white limo parked in front of the house, and in front of the limo were two smaller cars.

"I'll wait," he said. "In case."

"In case what?"

"In case he locks you out."

"Roger, I'm not going to let him."

"I'll still wait."

He could be as stubborn as she was.

Kristin knew he was behind her in the driveway, watching her every move. She knew, too, that if she rang the doorbell, she was asking for trouble. She decided that she might be lucky and find the door unlocked.

It was unlocked. She walked on into the house, waving cheerily to Roger as if she'd been admitted by Justin, and then closed the door softly behind her.

And there she was.

She stood still in the hallway for a minute, listening. There was laughter coming from the living room. Laughter, talking, the clink of ice against glasses. Some music was playing softly on the stereo. There was the definite feel of a party about the place.

She couldn't stand in the entryway all night. She moved forward, but hovered by the wall for a minute, trying to discern what she could about the people in the room.

Christina Anderson she recognized instantly from her newspaper photos. She had the kind of hair that slunk low over one eye, dark blond, sexy. She was tall and thin. Poised by the mantel, she looked more like a model or ingenue herself than an agent.

Artie Fein was just the opposite. He was a small man with graying hair, and the frazzled air of a C.P.A. during tax season. He was sitting on the sofa, looking as if he was falling asleep, beside a woman who had to be Sue's "twit." Roxanne did not resemble her pictures much. She was much thinner in person, very small, vulnerable looking. Her hair was long and soft and nearly platinum. Her eyes were sky blue, and she had a look of innocence about her that seemed to say she'd be perfect for a role in *Arsenic and Old Lace* once a few more years had passed her by.

She was pretty, though. Not sleek and beautiful like Christina, but very, very pretty. And she was watching

Justin, who sat across the room from her in one of the leather chairs, as if she could eat him up.

Kristin tried to associate the woman in front of her with the woman she had spoken with on the phone. It was difficult. In appearance, she was soft as clouds. On the phone, she had seemed very self-assured and confident, smooth, matter-of-fact, far more assertive than her fragile appearance would lead one to believe.

Kristin didn't have time to study her further, because a very handsome young blond man standing near Christina Anderson by the fire was looking her way, and smiling with definite interest. Jack Jones. She recognized him from his pictures, too.

"What have we here?" he said softly. "Come in, come in. Justin, you never told us what treasures you've been hiding out here in the country."

Justin hadn't been expecting any "treasures" that evening, that was obvious.

Of course he knew it had to be Kristin. Even before he stood and turned around and stared at her. His scowl was as dark and dangerous as thunderclouds.

"What the hell are you doing here?" Justin grated out.

"Never mind him," Jack Jones said, walking across the room to her. He took her hand. She glanced down at his. The skin was soft, the nails were immaculately manicured. She stared at him, wondering about him. Justin had said that he was happily married.

Justin had also said that there'd been a rumor floating about that he'd had an affair with Myra.

When he was in front of her, Jack lowered his voice instantly. "Be my date for the evening. My wife couldn't make it, and I'm bored silly with these folks. Don't let Justin's growl get to you. Who are you, by the way?"

"Her name is—Krissy Doria," Justin grated out, ad-libbing by way of introduction. Obviously, he didn't want anyone to know who she was. He knew that she had phoned Roxanne and obviously realized that she had probably given her name. "She's a—neighbor," he said flatly. He stared at her, still furious. "Well, do come on in then," he said more quietly.

Lethally quiet.

He began a round of introductions. Besides Jack Jones, Roxanne and the two agents, there was a handsome woman of about thirty-three, Maria Canova, the woman taking over Myra's role, and Harry Johnston, the dignified and fine character actor. He was as solicitous as Jack Jones.

"And what do you do, Miss Doria?" Artie Fein asked her, suddenly awake and interested. "You don't happen to be a young theater hopeful?" He was standing, reaching into his pocket. "I could put you to work modeling tomorrow, if you want. Here, take my card—"

"Artie!" Christina Anderson interrupted him. "Justin is my client, and Miss Doria is his friend. If she needs an agent, she can call me."

"Excuse them," Jack Jones said. "They do tend to act like children. It's nice to meet you. Are you a budding starlet? What do you do?"

Kristin didn't have a chance to answer because Justin did so for her. "I found her in the library," he said coolly. "And it's a wonderful place for her to be. She loves research."

"A librarian!" Roxanne sniffed. "Well, honey, close yourself away! It makes life better for the rest of us out there." She offered Kristin a gaze that was surprisingly warm and welcoming. Maybe she didn't consider Kristin any kind of serious competition. "Doria!" Roxanne continued. "You must be some relation to that nice young couple we interrupted earlier."

"Yes," Kristin said quickly, determined to answer something for herself. "He's my cousin."

"Cute little country cousins," Roxanne murmured.

"My, my," Jack murmured, "we do seem to have disrupted everyone. But you see, well, Maria was determined to come out as soon as she could after the storm. And if Maria was coming, well, I'm in debt to Justin. His play gave me my first big break, so I had to come, too. And Harry never likes to miss a party, and Roxanne can't stand to be left out of one. So here we are."

"How nice," Kristin said. She opened her mouth to speak again, then quickly closed it. Justin suddenly had an arm around her. A tight arm around her. "All right, so I've been trying to keep her from the dangerous likes of you, Jack. And you, too, Harry. As it happens, originally, I dug the lady out of the snow. She was all ice at first, but she has thawed rather nicely. She plays chess brilliantly, and we've become very good friends. And I think that it's running late for her, and I'm exhausted myself. You all surprised the hell out of me, showing up tonight. So who's staying here, and who's at the inn?"

"If you've got a room, Justin, Roxanne and I can share," Maria Canova said in a husky feminine voice that was mature, pleasing ... and very sexy.

"And of course," Roxanne added. "Ms. Doria is welcome with us, too. And Christina."

"I'm at the inn, folks," Christina said, grinning. "Sleeping till noon. I'll be back tomorrow afternoon, though. We'll do something quaint together."

Something quaint. Kristin decided she didn't like Justin's agent.

"Ms. Doria?" Roxanne asked.

"Ms. Doria sleeps with me," Justin said firmly.

Kristin had thought she was prepared for anything he might choose to throw out that night, but she wasn't. She felt the color flooding to her cheeks.

So much so that she almost forgot to watch the others for reactions. She recalled that she should just in time and looked around.

Jack laughed out loud. Harry cleared his throat. Artie merely looked aside. Maria seemed cool as a cucumber.

But both Roxanne and Christina seemed to gain color. Their plastic smiles remained in place, though, and there was little that Kristin could tell from their reactions.

"Ah, well, can I have my old room back?" Jack asked Justin, breaking the sudden silence that Justin's last comment had brought on. "The one down at the far end of the hall. There are twin beds in it, Harry. You staying? Or Artie, how about you? Everybody seems to have a roommate."

"I called for a room at the inn," Harry said. "I spend enough time with you young delinquents."

"I can drive you back," Christina offered.

"I guess I'll stay here," Artie decided.

"Good," Justin said. His hands were still on Kristin's shoulders, holding her close against him. "Make yourselves at home. Help yourselves to whatever you need. You all know the place well enough. Christina, you and Harry are welcome to stay, too. All the closets upstairs have clean linens. But if you'd really rather not, see yourselves out. We don't lock our doors here often, not in the quaint countryside. But anyway, excuse Krissy and me, will you? We're turning in."

"Krissy" couldn't protest. His hands on her were like iron clamps. He steered her around and toward the stairs. And when they reached them, he prodded her up.

At the top of the stairway, he steered her to the left. And Kristin kept silent while he pushed her through the doorway to his suite's sitting room, but as soon as the door had closed behind them, she broke free and spun around.

"That's enough!"

"That's enough!" he repeated furiously, advancing on her. "I told you not to come!"

"If you don't want me here, what the hell are you doing dragging me off up to your bedroom?"

He stepped back, a mocking curl forming at the corner of his lip. His eyes moved slowly over the length of her. "Hell, honey, if you're going to be here, you might as well be useful," he commented dryly.

"Oh, you son of a—" Kristin began, but he dragged her suddenly back into his arms. His hand landed over her mouth, hard.

His whisper touched her ear. "Shush!"

She wanted to kick him, hard. But she felt the pounding of his heart along with the pressure of his touch, and she held still.

Then she heard the soft rapping against the door. "Justin! Justin, are you in there."

"Yeah. Yeah. Be with you in a second!" he called out.

"You shut up!" he warned Kristin with a whisper. "And don't think of leaving these rooms. Don't you realize you could be in danger here?"

He thrust her away from him. "Get in the bedroom!"

"I will not—!"

"You will!"

And she did, because he hiked her over his shoulder, walked into the bedroom and tossed her ignominiously down upon the bed. She tried to scramble up, but he was already walking out. He closed the door behind him.

Kristin leaped up and hurried across the room. She placed her ear against the door. She could hear Justin. He had opened the door to the hallway.

"Roxanne! What is it?"

"Justin, I had to let you know. That's why I came. There's some woman hounding me about the story again."

"Yeah?"

"A reporter. She called this morning. She's trying to rehash the whole murder thing again. Justin, I wonder what she knows. I don't know what to tell her, what to try to hide."

Kristin leaned against the wall. If she knows what? she wanted to shout. She held still, her heart thundering. What was Justin hiding?

"Thanks for your concern, Roxanne. But there will be lots of reporters asking questions now that the show is opening again. Talk to them. See them."

"But Justin—"

"Roxanne, what can I say?"

Kristin didn't know what he could say, because Roxanne's next words were whispered.

And Justin's next words were said more softly, too.

She heard Roxanne's next comment. "Oh, Justin, I'd do anything for you. Anything. You know that."

Kristin gritted her teeth. Sure. Justin knew exactly what she'd do for him, and now Kristin knew, too. She couldn't believe the woman—when she knew that Justin already had someone in his bedroom!

Not that it would mean anything. Not tonight.

Kristin didn't hear anything else except for the door closing softly. She hurried away from the bedroom door and sat at the foot of the bed. Then she realized that she didn't want to be there and she leaped to her feet and hurried across the room to the window.

She was certain her hair was still flying when Justin entered the bedroom. Her heart was still pounding a hundred miles a minute.

He glanced at her irritably. "I know damned well that you were listening at the door. Go ahead. Sit down. Gasp," he added dryly.

She shook her head. She hadn't the air to speak.

"You're going home first thing in the morning," he told her. "For now, get to bed."

"I'll be fine on the couch."

She gasped with a far greater urgency when he moved impatiently across the floor again, lifted her and dropped her onto the bed. He towered over her there. "I don't know about you, but I need some sleep. And I won't get it with you sitting in a chair. In the morning, you go straight home."

He started stripping off his clothing. Kristin turned on her back, her heart pounding hard again. One minute he was pulling her to him; the next, he was pushing her away.

He crawled into the bed beside her. "Take off that ridiculous dress," he told her.

"A true romantic!" Kristin said sarcastically, inching away from him. "What a way with women. No wonder they throw themselves at you, Mr. Magnasun. Or is it Mountjoy tonight? Does anyone in this house tonight go by his or her right name? If I go into the theater, is Krissy Doria my stage name?"

He groaned, and before she knew it, he had pushed her beneath him. "Take off that ridiculous dress!" he repeated harshly. Then he added slowly and with emphasis, "The dress is not ridiculous. The fact that you're wearing it in a bed where you've been with me naked at least a dozen times is totally ridiculous. I had to make up a name for you, and you know exactly why." He was still on top of her, but now he was up on his knees, helping her off with her dress—whether she wanted it off or not. He was slipping it over her head. And he wasn't neat with it. He just let it fall to the floor.

"Justin, if you think—" she began furiously.

But he tossed the covers over her, and lay down beside her.

Kristin flushed. He didn't think anything. She was the one assuming that they'd have sex if they lay naked together.

"I think we're going to sleep. And that you're getting out of here tomorrow."

"Justin, damn you, I can discover things—"

"Like what? What have you learned tonight?"

Nothing. Except that he might be hiding something from her.

"I learned that Roxanne Baynes would sleep with you at the drop of a pin," she said coolly, holding the covers to her chest.

"That doesn't make her a murderer."

"It gives her a motive. She wanted to get rid of your wife."

"Estranged wife."

"Where was Myra sleeping while she was here and still . . ."

"Breathing?" Justin said softly. "She had her own room—down the hall that way. See, you haven't learned anything. Not anything at all."

"Yes, I have. Since the critic, Joseph Banks, didn't seem to feel that he had to join this party, that very well might eliminate him and his wife as suspects."

"It might. It might not. He may just be smart enough not to return to the scene of the crime."

Kristin pulled the covers over her shoulders and rolled away from him. She lay as close to the edge of the bed as she could.

"You don't know a damned thing," he said harshly. "And you're not going to risk trying to find out anything, either!"

"Oh, go to—"

"What?"

"I said, I already know who did it," Kristin mumbled.

"Who?"

"The butler. The damned butler did it. Isn't that always the way in a play?"

Justin was silent for a moment. Then she heard his sigh. "It's a damned pity I didn't have a butler. It would have been convenient if the butler had done it."

He rose, padded over to the light and turned it off. Kristin felt him come back to the bed in the darkness. She felt him slip beneath the covers.

Then she didn't hear anything, or feel anything.

Not until...

His whisper just at the lobe of her ear.

"Do you know 'who done it' every time the butler didn't 'do it'?" he asked.

She smothered back a startled gasp as she turned toward him in the nearly total darkness.

"The husband, Kristin. The husband. Every damn time."

By the time she blinked, he had moved away. She swallowed hard.

Not this time, dear God, not this time! she thought.

No, not this time.

Chapter 11

When she awoke, Kristin found she was lying at the edge of the bed with the covers pulled tightly to her chin. She lay still for a moment, then she cautiously rolled over.

Justin was on his own side of the bed, on the edge, his naked back to her.

For a moment she was tempted to touch him. To run her fingers over the broad expanse of bronze flesh. She really was in love with him, she thought. Deeply in love with him. But he was doing his very best to be rude and obnoxious to her. He wanted her out of his house. He planned to get rid of her this morning.

He wasn't going to get rid of her, no matter how horrible he chose to be. He could say anything that he wanted.

She hadn't originally come for a story, but now she was going to get one. And she was going to prove him innocent in the process, and then he could follow her back to Boston, crawling in the snow, to apologize.

If he really loved her, too.

She bit her lip. She wasn't going to touch him now.

She rose as quietly as she could and tiptoed into the elegant master bath. She kept her eyes from the marble whirlpool and headed straight for the shower stall. She turned the water on cold, to wake herself up, and she showered quickly. Then she wrapped herself in a towel and returned to the bedroom, gingerly, silently, picking up her clothes. He didn't move while she dressed.

But when she put her hand on the doorknob, he spoke to her at last. "Where do you think you're going?"

"Downstairs. I'm dying for a cup of coffee."

"You're going home. Have your cup of coffee. I'll be down in ten minutes to take you. Be ready."

Kristin paused. She wondered if she shouldn't stay, curl up beside him and try to convince him that she wasn't going home.

No. He'd just let her get carried away and he'd enjoy every minute of it. And then he'd take her home.

She wanted the few minutes she was going to have alone.

She hurried downstairs. She heard voices in the kitchen, and she followed the sound, trying to form some kind of a plan. It wasn't easy with only ten minutes stretching before her.

Play it by ear, she thought.

Brilliant idea. It was her only choice.

She stepped into the kitchen. Maria was at the table with Artie, and Jack was standing by one of the window seats, looking out on the snow. Roxanne was by the coffeepot, and Christina and Harry had apparently just arrived because they were taking off their coats in the sun room.

"Good morning, Ms. Doria!" Christina called out to her cheerfully. "What a late group! I had thought we might want to prowl the countryside for a little village restaurant for lunch, and I find this crowd just groping around for coffee. Tell me, is my talented young client awake yet?"

"Yes, he's awake. He should be down in a few minutes."

"It's far too early for lunch," Maria said with a yawn. She was staring off through the living room, and she flashed Kristin a wry smile. "As for me, I'm going swimming. I've never been in the water in winter. It looks almost decadent."

"What do you think, Ms. Doria?" Roxanne asked in a soft drawl.

Kristin shrugged, determined to appear undaunted. "The water is very nice. Warm."

"It must cost a bundle to heat," Artie said.

"But my clients make very good money," Christina advised him sweetly.

"I'm for a walk!" Jack announced. "Nice clean, cold country air. We don't see much of that in the city, do we?"

Harry sniffed. "The Big Apple is not that bad. There are days like this there."

"A New Yorker born and bred," Roxanne said. "Harry's from the Bronx," she told Kristin, bringing her a cup of black coffee. "He lost the accent doing summer stock for years and years and years, isn't that right, Harry? You'll never convince him that the world outside Manhattan and the boroughs really exists at all."

"I am most certainly aware that the world exists beyond New York!" Harry said with dignity, then he smiled in a friendly way at Kristin. "Very aware! In fact, I wouldn't mind seeing your little library, Ms. Doria."

Kristin decided this was it, her grand opening to make her move. "I'm not a librarian," she told him, taking a seat at the table and spooning sugar and cream into her coffee.

"No?" Harry said.

She shook her head. "I'm a reporter."

The room was silent. Dead silent. Kristin realized she virtually could have heard a pin drop. And she surely had center stage. They were all staring at her.

"A reporter?" Jack said.

"Oh, my Lord!" Roxanne drawled. "You're the woman who called me!"

Kristin nodded.

"But I thought you said your name was . . . oh. Kristin. But wasn't it Kristin Kennedy?"

"There's a nom de plume in there somewhere," Christina murmured. Kristin didn't correct her.

Jack started to laugh. "Still want to see the library, Harry?"

"Wait a minute, please! I'm not here to malign anyone!" Kristin insisted. "But you all must believe in Justin's innocence, or you wouldn't be here."

"Not necessarily," Jack said dryly. "Some of us just may feel that the old boy had the right to do her in."

"He didn't kill her," Kristin insisted.

"And here we have another member of his fan club," Roxanne murmured.

"Justin does have that effect on women," Christina murmured.

Did he have it on her? Kristin wondered. Then she wondered if she should have made her announcement so casually. They were a group. They knew one another. They might be disassociated in their real lives once the play wasn't going on, but in this, they were a solid group.

The group that had been together when Myra Breckenridge was killed.

And one of them had done it.

It felt just a little bit as if it was them—against her.

It felt as if . . . ! *It was.* But how on earth could anyone ever discover who had hated Myra enough to kill her?

A little chill snaked down her spine. There might be a way to draw a killer out. A very rash way.

She would be putting herself into danger to do it. Grave danger.

But was there any other way?

"You see," Kristin threw out boldly, "I think I just may know the truth. I'm a researcher. I dig really deep. Justin did find me in a library."

Once again, you could almost hear a pin drop.

"Then who—" Maria began.

"Not one of us!" Jack insisted.

"You want to interview us, right?" Harry said suddenly. "Make certain that your idea is correct?"

"Yes, of course."

"But Justin is innocent?" Roxanne murmured.

"That's right. I keep thinking—"

"Think all you want!" a male voice interrupted suddenly. Harsh, cold. Justin's voice. He was standing behind Kristin with her coat in his hand. "But don't think it here. Say goodbye to the nice people, Kristin. I'm taking you home."

How much of what she had said had he heard? Kristin wondered.

"Oh, now Justin, don't be churlish," Jack said.

"Churlish?" Roxanne murmured.

"He's been doing too much Shakespeare or something," Harry told her. "But Justin, really, we don't mind that Ms. Doria—er—Ms. Kennedy here is a reporter. Really, we don't.''

"I do," Justin said pointedly. "Come on, Kristin."

The chair scraped against the floor as he pulled it away from the table. He grabbed her hand. And she sensed that if she decided to have it out right there, he'd be more than ready to drag her out physically. She was really no match for him.

She jumped up and circled around the table. "Justin, you really can be rude, you know. I can't leave just yet. I've—I've got to pick up a few things. In the bedroom. Excuse me."

She was certain that he would have caught her by the roots of her hair if he could have done so, but she slipped around the table and hurried for the stairs. Then she ran up them as quickly as she could. She had barely reached the sitting room before he caught up with her.

"Justin—"

He pushed the door open and they were both inside. He slammed the door shut and looked at her as if he were ready to shake her hard.

Or throttle her.

But she knew his temper. Standing on her toes, she ran her fingers over his collar. "Justin, I had to talk to you alone. Give me a chance! I'll be careful...." she began huskily. She pressed close to him. She meant to tease and torment.

And it seemed that she did. He sighed softly, and he kissed her. Kissed her hard. The kind of kiss that seared to her soul and left her quivering and with hot little ripples dancing along her spine.

Then he pushed her away from him. "No!"

He grabbed her arm and led her—no, dragged her—out of the room. She had to step quickly to keep up with his pace as he led her back down the stairs and to the door.

"Kristin?"

Christina and Artie appeared from the kitchen. Then the others were all there, too.

"Say goodbye, Kristin," Justin told her.

She smiled over gritted teeth. "Goodbye. It was lovely to meet you all. And I'm sure we will meet again."

"Oh, we will, we will!" Jack said cheerfully.

They all gave her big hugs, as if they were telling a relative goodbye after too short a stay.

"Maybe he'll let you come back for breakfast tomorrow," Artie told her. "I do all kinds of literary work, too, you know."

"Well, I don't write novels—"

"You may one day."

"Yeah. Myra's murder would make a great whodunit," Jack supplied dryly.

"Maybe I will write a book—" Kristin began to say to Artie.

"Jack, thanks for the vote of confidence. Artie, Kristin is taking you for a ride. She's quite good at it."

"And other things, too, so it seems," Roxanne observed lightly.

Kristin gritted her teeth again, looking at her. Roxanne's wide-eyed innocence was in full swing.

"Be a good girl and let's go and maybe I will let you come back for breakfast," Justin said.

There was another flurry of goodbyes, of kisses on her cheek. Kristin felt something brush her hand, and realized that she was now holding a piece of paper. A piece of paper that someone must have slipped to her. She closed her fingers over it.

Justin helped her into her coat, then opened the front door.

Roxanne smiled like the Cheshire cat, watching her leave.

And then Kristin was out in the snow and Justin was dragging her to his car. She was barely in it before he slammed the door, and walked around to the driver's side.

"Take me to my car," she told him primly.

"No way. I'll take you to Roger's."

"Then Roger will just have to take me to my car. I've been thrown out. Now let me at least get my own transportation."

He ignored her. Within minutes they were driving up in front of Roger and Sue's. Justin stepped out to open her door and deposit her on the front step.

"Don't come back!" he told her.

She closed her fingers more tightly over the piece of paper. She smiled demurely. "It will be a cold day in hell when I come back to you, Mr. Magnasun."

"All of these seem to be cold days in hell lately," he muttered.

"Thanks."

"I didn't mean you. Oh, hell, maybe I do mean you! Now stay home."

He gave her a sharp blue stare to emphasize that he meant his words. Kristin just kept smiling. He turned and left her at last.

She waited until the Land Rover had disappeared down the road. Then she looked down at her hand and slowly opened her fingers. It was just a torn piece of napkin.

But scrawled on it was a message.

Meet me in the copse in the far rear of Justin's property. Today. Noon. Alone. I could be in danger. I'll give you the story.

There was no signature. But the script had been penned with flourishes. As if it had been written by a woman.

Roxanne?

Kristin closed her fingers around the piece of paper, and felt both excitement and anxiety sweep through her.

Very soon, she was certain, she would know who had really killed Myra.

Alone...

She'd be a fool to go alone. If she didn't, though, she'd never discover the truth. Maybe she could get Roger to help her.... No. Sue would have a fit, saying that Kristin could get them both killed. And she could. And then Roger's brand-new little embryo wouldn't have a father.

No, she couldn't involve Roger.

But she didn't even have her own car.

In the midst of her ponderings, she saw a car coming down the road. She walked closer to the embankment, watching. Then a smile touched her face and she started to wave wildly.

It was Miss Petrie from the library. And she was happy to give Kristin a ride back to her car.

When he returned from dropping Kristin off, Justin sat in his car in front of the house, tapping his fingers against the wheel.

Kristin. What was he going to do with her? She was so foolishly reckless, taking so many chances. And with every moment they were together, he realized more and more how deeply he was falling in love with her. She was very much like a dream—his own special dream—coming true. She belonged in the house, and she belonged with him. With her boundless energy and endless faith, those shimmering eyes, the warmth she exuded...

She could be in danger. He could be in danger himself because the real killer was probably in his house....

He leaned his head back and closed his eyes. Through the years, he had gone over the night again and again. He had never been able to decide who the killer might be.

But one thing he was sure of. The way Kristin was poking around, she had to be making the killer very nervous.

He got out of the car and hurried back up to the house. The entry was empty, as were the living room and the kitchen. He didn't see anybody, except Maria Canova.

She was stretched out on one of the floats in the pool, wearing a bathing suit and sunglasses, and sipping a drink. She patted the float and invited him in to join her.

"No, thanks."

"The water is wonderful."

"I know. It's just not a novelty to me any longer." He paused a moment. "Where's everyone else?"

"Who are you looking for?" Maria asked him. Her voice had dropped an octave, it seemed. Her smile was damned practiced. "I mean, was there a particular reason you were so anxious to take your little friend home?"

"Actually, yes, there was a reason that I took her home. I love her, and I don't want anything to happen to her," he said bluntly.

"Well, then, she should watch her step," Maria said idly.

"What does that mean?"

"Well, she announced this morning that she knew who the real killer was."

"Excuse me, will you, Maria?" Justin said curtly. "I've got a few things to do."

Frustrated, startled, worried and angry, he turned away from her and went back into the house and into his office.

You little fool! he thought. He sat at his desk, reaching for the phone. And then he paused. You're playing with fire, when all I'm trying to do is protect you! Oh, Kristin, take care.

I love you....

It was so very true. He was in love with Kristin. And he loved her. There were those subtle differences. He was in love with her because the mere scent of her perfume could excite him. A glance in her eyes could trigger his desire, a soft sigh from her lips made him feel as if the world had taken on a new spin. When she walked into a room, his breath caught. His heart took on a new beat. He wanted her so badly he had barely been able to lie by her side without touching her last night.

He was in love.

Twenty, forty years from now, he might not feel that same sweet flash of shimmering excitement every time she spoke. His desires could wane with age.

But his love for her never would.

And there, the subtle difference. He loved her for her wide trusting gray eyes. For the way she thought, for the way she spoke. He loved her for the way that she stood by him. He even loved her for being so damned stubborn. He loved her for the way she cared about her cousin, for the way she was with people. Perhaps she wouldn't always be so trusting, but she was honest and level. And he knew that every word she had said to him was the truth. She had never come for a story. She had just stumbled onto him.

And he had stumbled onto her. After Myra, after being convinced that there was no truth in the world.

She was beautiful. So very beautiful with her rich dark hair and dark-lashed gray eyes and supple form. But she offered so much more, too.

"I hope I get to tell you," he murmured. He picked up the phone and began to dial. It wasn't something that he meant to say over the phone. He just wanted to make sure that she had gotten in okay.

Sue answered the phone.

"Hello, Sue. It's Justin. Let me speak to Kristin."

"What do you mean?" Sue said on a note of rising anxiety.

"Sue, I need to speak with her—"

"She's not here. She's been with you since last night, hasn't she?"

"I let her off at your house more than an hour ago."

"Well, she didn't come in. Oh, Justin—"

"Don't worry, Sue. I'll find her."

He hung up before she could say more, or get herself any more worried.

Kristin could be anywhere, he told himself. Anywhere at all. She had probably gotten a ride, and gone for her car. She was so damned stubborn. She was on her way back here. Any minute she'd ring the doorbell.

No, she wouldn't. He didn't understand it, but dread was sweeping through him with such a vengeance that he seemed paralyzed for a moment. He stood, tense—frightened half out of his wits.

She was in danger.

How did he know? Intuition . . .

Or the mere fact that she had been playing with a murderer?

And even more. If Kristin had gone somewhere without telling him or Sue, she had to know that one of them would have stopped her if possible. She had to be out there somewhere, playing with fire.

He looked out on the yard. It was snowing again. Big, soft flakes. The kind that obliterated footprints. The kind that had been falling the night Myra died.

And there was more. There was someone moving in the snow. Walking quickly, furtively. Heading for the forest behind the house.

Maybe there was nothing wrong. Maybe someone was just going for a walk....

No. There was something going on. No one walked along in such a hurry, shoulders hunched, looking over their shoulders in such a way unless they were up to something. Unless they were on their way to some kind of clandestine meeting.

"Damn!" he swore out loud. Kristin was missing. Kristin had thrown out words just as if she were throwing out bait. And now she might well be meeting with someone out there in the forest.

He grabbed a jacket and hurried for the stairs. He raced through the house to the back, throwing open the door to the elements.

"Hey!" Maria called from the pool as the cold blast of wintry air swept into the glass enclosure.

He ignored her.

Parked at the bottom of the rolling slope was Kristin's Cherokee.

And the figure in the snow had disappeared.

Wherever she was, Kristin was meeting the murderer.

Justin started to run.

From the cover of the trees, Kristin watched the figure coming closer and closer.

At first, she had barely been able to see the person. The snow had started to fall again. She felt the tension and fear sizzling through her, and she tried to judge the size of the person. She wasn't small herself. Five foot eight and a fairly strong 130 pounds. She could take care of herself fairly well if only her opponent wasn't . . .

As strong as the person who had killed Myra Breckenridge. That was the only person who might want to strangle her now.

The figure was small, she judged at last. Certainly no larger than she was.

And then, through the snow and the trees, the figure appeared.

"Kristin!" Her name was called in a soft, sibilant hiss. She felt an eerie unease sweeping up the length of her spine. As if someone had run their nails over a blackboard.

Again the voice called her. "Kristin!"

Kristin stepped from the trees.

And came face-to-face with Roxanne Baynes.

"I'm here," she said softly, keeping her fingers in the pockets of her coat. It was all that she could do. Was Roxanne going to wind her fingers around her neck?

"Oh, thank God!" Roxanne said. "And you came alone!"

"Yes," Kristin said uneasily.

But Roxanne seemed even more nervous than Kristin was. She kept looking around the snow-covered landscape. "I had to write that note to you so quickly! I ran into the living room and did it when you were upstairs. I had the strangest feeling that someone was watching me, but when I turned around, I was alone. And I'm not sure if anyone saw me give it to you or not. I tried to be careful. And when I left the house...oh, I hope I wasn't followed."

Kristin looked around herself. "Maybe we shouldn't be meeting out here."

"Oh, but nobody must know that I know! Not until you can prove it! He'll kill me!"

Wary, Kristin knit her brows. "Who?"

"It was Jack. Jack Jones."

"Jones? Why? Was he really having an affair with Myra? I thought that he was a happily married man."

Roxanne shook her head vehemently. "Jack is happy with lots and lots of people, and he is certainly not a discriminatory lover! He goes for any race, color, creed and even sex. See, I can't prove this. I've been afraid to say anything. Because if he murdered her, he won't think twice about murdering me!"

"But still, why would he murder Myra? Was an affair worth killing for?"

"Roxanne!"

The girl's name rang out. Both Kristin and Roxanne jerked around.

A second figure was hurrying toward them across the snow. Huffing and puffing.

It was Jack. Jack Jones.

"I didn't do it!" he cried out, scrambling over the white drifts to reach them. "She did it!" he cried to Kristin. "She did it! She was dying to get her hands on Justin, and Justin hadn't divorced Myra. And Myra had a way of making people furious."

"Oh, my Lord!" Roxanne gasped, coming around from behind Kristin. "You did see my note. You were watching me in the kitchen."

"I did not see your note! I saw you leaving the house. And I knew damned well you'd be trying to get to Ms. Kennedy—to lay it all on me! You had much more to gain than I did!"

"Jack Jones, I did not do it!" Roxanne insisted. "You did it. Because you quit seeing Myra to spend more time with your lover, Thomas Schiff! Myra was furious. And she was blackmailing you, saying that she'd tell your wife—"

"My wife knows!" Jack insisted, red-faced. He looked at Kristin. "We've an agreement, she and I. We have children, so we keep up a marriage. And Myra was trying to blackmail me. But I didn't kill her."

Great, Kristin thought. So much for the great and dramatic confrontation. She had two killers. . . .

Or none.

Well, she decided, this had been a waste of time.

Then she frowned suddenly. About twenty feet deeper into the forest was a strangely shaped shadow. Was there someone hiding behind that tree?

There were footprints in the snow around the tree.

Maybe someone else had seen Roxanne write her note. Maybe that someone had come here to listen and learn.

She studied the shadow again, then nearly laughed out loud. The shadow was crooked because the tree was crooked. But the footprints . . .

Who else was in the wood?

Neither Roxanne nor Jack seemed to be paying any attention as she walked away from them. Even as she moved the twenty or thirty feet closer to the clump of trees, she could hear them arguing.

Well, maybe the afternoon wouldn't be such a waste after all. She felt fairly certain she could eliminate two suspects—Jack and Roxanne. If one of them really was a killer, the other would be dead by now.

She paused before the first footprint. It wasn't very clear, but there was a long trail of footprints. She began to follow them excitedly, seeing that they became more and more defined and clearly etched in the snow as she moved into the copse of trees.

She came to a stop by a tree and a very clear print.

The cold seemed to sweep around her as she did so. She was chilled inside and out as she stared at the footprint. It was large. A heavy snow boot.

A sudden sound startled her. It was a sneeze, she realized, and she looked up.

A sneeze . . .

The person who had made the footprint was still beside the tree. Not two steps away from her.

Staring at her.

The person . . .

The killer. Skulking out in the woods. He had been the one to see Roxanne writing her note in the kitchen. And he was here now. She knew that he was the killer. She knew because the truth was so naked in his eyes as he stood there, staring at her.

"So you have stumbled upon me. I was hoping not to have to hurt you," the killer said wearily.

"Kristin!"

She heard her name shouted. Hope soared in her heart. It was Justin.

She spun around, ready to scream to him. My God, she had come so far! She hadn't realized how far she had wandered into the woods.

But Justin was coming. He was running across the snow, floundering, running again. He didn't see her there in the trees. He just seemed to know that she was out there, somewhere.

Black-jeaned and black-jacketed, he was racing through the snow. He had nearly reached Jack and Roxanne. He was so very, very close. All that she had to do was scream, and he would see her.

Sound never left her throat. She had found the killer, and the killer had found her.

A jacket was thrown over her head, hands clamped hard over her throat, choking her words.

She struggled fiercely, but she was dragged deeper into the shadow of the trees.

She couldn't breathe. Desperately, she tried to inhale. She fought against the fingers that held a death grip around her throat.

But the white of the day was turning black. Don't! she told herself. Please, please, don't lose consciousness! she commanded herself.

No, please...

Dear God, Justin hadn't even seen her. Neither Jack nor Roxanne had seen her leave....

She couldn't stop fighting. She was being dragged through the forest. She had to fight for awareness.

He was strong....

They went a fair distance. She was lifted, thrown. She was in a car, she realized dimly. The jacket was pressed down upon her, suffocating her.

But her fingers ceased to fight the hold upon her throat.

And the blackness descended surely upon her.

Chapter 12

Kristin had been mistaken about one thing. Justin had seen her.

One minute she was there, moving through the trees. The next second, it seemed, she had disappeared.

"Where the hell is Kristin!" he screamed as he reached Jack and Roxanne.

"Justin, she's right here—" Roxanne began, turning around. "Well, she was right here."

"No, she wandered off into the trees. She seemed to be looking at something," Jack said. "Justin, do you want me to—"

"Damn right! Look for her!" Justin snapped. He tore through the forest, then paused, his heart beating. He screamed her name, his hands clenched by his side. "Kristin!" There was no answer, just the mocking whisper of the winter wind.

Then he realized there were two sets of footprints before him. Two...

He started to follow them, running quickly.

Tree by tree.

Then, suddenly, there were no longer two sets of footprints. There was one set of prints....

And then deep grooves in the snow. As if something had been dragged through it.

Something, or someone.

His heart quickened. He almost screamed out her name again.

Then he saw that he had reached the embankment at the edge of the copse. The road was beneath him.

And there was a car down on that road.

"Justin!" Jack was behind him.

"Call the sheriff!" Justin said.

They could both see Kristin.

Someone was lifting her lifeless body into the back seat of the car.

Lifeless.

Oh, dear God, no!

"No!"

He whispered the word in agony, and he started to run again. "Tell the sheriff to look for the car!" he called.

The killer was already in the driver's seat. And the car was already being revved to life.

Justin ran....

The car began to move.

He had to keep it in sight. It was his only hope to save Kristin. The sheriff would never arrive in time.

Just as the car disappeared around the bend in the road, he took a flying leap off the embankment and onto the road. He fell to his knees on the icy pavement.

Teeth clenched, Justin stumbled to his feet. He'd lost his gloves. His hands were bleeding, raw. He ignored his hands, and started to run down the road after the car.

Run, run, into the snow. The dazzling white snow. His lungs were bursting. His eyes stung from the cold.

Please, please, let her be alive! Let me reach her! he prayed in silence.

He could only run so much farther.

Kristin awoke, feeling herself being dragged across the snow again. She opened her eyes, then closed them quickly. She had no idea where she was. If she feigned unconsciousness, she might manage to regain some strength and run.

No.

She heard a voice, a handsome, fine, dignified voice.

"It's no good, Ms. Kennedy. I know you're awake. It won't do you any good. From the moment you made your announcement this morning, I knew I had to get to you to shut you up. At first I thought you were another Myra, that you could be paid off. But I'd paid her blackmail for so long."

Kristin opened her eyes.

She looked into the distinguished features of Mr. Harry Johnston, renowned character actor. He had both her hands, and was dragging her backward over the snow. He paused when she looked at him.

"You'll be very weak for a long time," he warned her. "I nearly killed you where we were."

"Why didn't you?" She was weak. Her throat burned. Her flesh was sore, probably bruising now. Did it matter? she wondered.

"I didn't have time to do a thorough job of it. And I...I don't mean to be crass, but I needed a better place to dispose of your body."

"Justin—" It was hard to speak. "Justin saw you take me!" she managed to whisper. It was a lie, but perhaps it would help.

He shook his head. "No, I'm sorry. We both know that that isn't true."

She had to find the strength to speak. "Harry, they'll know it was you this time! It wasn't Justin, Roxanne or Jack. Harry, they'd run out of suspects quickly!"

"Proof," Harry said softly. "They need proof." He sat down on a rock behind her, not vicious. He was truly regretful. "I didn't want to hurt you. I saw Roxanne writing that note, and I knew I had to try and find out what she was going to say. I watched her, and I came around the back way to the woods. I was hoping you really didn't know anything. I meant to listen, nothing more. But then I saw your face, and I saw in your eyes that you knew it was me. And I knew you would find a way to prove it."

She grated her teeth, shivering. He went on talking.

"You know, it's a hard business, Ms. Kennedy. I never meant to kill Myra. But she planned to ruin me."

"How?" Kristin asked, amazed as well as terrified. She had been so certain that Roxanne had somehow done it.

"I drink, Miss Kennedy."

"So do a lot of people. Alcoholism is a disease. Why wouldn't you get help? Why kill someone?"

"Ah, in my case, I was on my very last chance. The director of *Snowfire* had promised that I would be out on my rear if he ever heard I'd taken a mouthful during the show. He gave me a chance. I had a, er, well, a moment of weakness. Myra found out about it. I'd never have stepped on a Broadway stage again if Myra had told the director what she found out. It was really very serious.

"I went off the wagon the first week of rehearsals. I had to go to the hospital to dry out. I lied to the director, saying I'd caught pneumonia. Myra found out from one of the nurses at the hospital. And she wasn't just blackmailing me. She was playing with me. She didn't really need money. She just liked having me in her power. And she was losing Justin. Well, she had lost him. Everyone else knew that, Maybe not Myra. So she'd blackmail me, then she'd say that she was going to tell anyway.

"That night, I followed her out into the snow. It was really coming down. I had on gloves, and the snow would eliminate any footprints. Still, I never meant to kill her. She made me mad and the next thing I knew I had my hands on the scarf she was wearing around her throat and then . . . well, then, the rest is history, right? But you knew that."

He stared at Kristin and then laughed. "You didn't know that. But you convinced me that you did. Well, I should be sorry. I guess I am."

"How can you kill me? You'll be caught this time! And you're not angry with me. How can you kill so easily?" Kristin demanded.

Where was she? They'd been in a car. But how far had they driven? How long had she been out? Even if she was right, and he was caught, what good would it do her?

She had known her meeting in the copse would be dangerous. She'd told Miss Petrie to call the sheriff, since she had decided not to involve Roger. But it hadn't been enough. . . .

It seemed that she was going to die anyway.

All that she could see around her were trees and snow and rocks. From somewhere near she could hear the sound of running water.

"I see that you can hear the water," he said softly, watching her eyes. "There's a stream nearby."

"And?" she asked.

"It runs into a very beautiful—and very deep—pond."

Kristin felt ill. She knew now what he planned to do. He would weight her body and toss it into the pond, and it would never appear again.

"How can you—?" she started to ask. She couldn't continue.

"I guess we all just get jaded," Harry said. "We just get jaded. They'll never be able to prove that I killed you, Ms. Kennedy."

"If you strangle me like you did Myra—" Kristin began.

"If they ever find your body, perhaps then they would have a case. But they won't."

She was weak, very weak. But she had to take a chance and run. She tried to struggle to her feet.

"No, no, Ms. Kennedy. You're not going anywhere."

From his pocket, Harry produced a gun. "I always try to be prepared. It's an actor's best asset."

She had Mace in her own pocket, Kristin thought.

Not fair...

Life wasn't fair. It had made Harry jaded. So jaded that he thought he could produce a gun and erase her life without a moment's remorse.

Harry cocked the gun and pointed it at Kristin.

"Hey, Johnston! Harry Johnston!"

They both started as they heard his name called.

Harry fired into the trees in the direction the voice was coming from.

"You missed, Johnston! You missed. Try again!"

Harry fired again, wildly. It was Justin calling, and they both knew it.

Justin was near. Very near.

Harry fired again. Just once.

Then a dark blur sped out of the trees, leaping high and landing hard on Harry's gun arm.

And Justin and Harry went down, deep down into the snow.

They rolled and rolled. Kristin fought hard for the strength to stand. She could see something glittering in the white expanse on the ground.

Glittering like...

Snowfire.

It was the gun. Harry's gun. She tried to reach it. Tried and tried. Inching toward it. Her fingers touched it. Slowly, slowly they closed around it.

Harry and Justin fought on.

She managed to get the gun into her hand. Exhausted, she rolled to her back.

She looked up, a scream forming in her throat as she realized there was silence now. And a tall figure was standing over her.

"It's all right," Justin said. He reached down and took the gun from her, then knelt by her side, sweeping her into his arms.

She tried to smile. "Harry...?"

"He's out cold."

"What if he awakens?" she demanded anxiously.

"I've got his hands tied up fairly well with his belt. He's not going anywhere. Anyway, I don't think he'll try. He knows it's all over now."

"But what will we do with him?"

"The sheriff will be coming. I told Jack to call him."

"He should already be coming," Kristin whispered weakly. "I asked Miss Petrie to call him when she dropped me off to get my car."

He grinned. "So you were smart about one thing. But you were stupid not to have waited."

"But I was meeting Roxanne," she said lamely. "I had to hear what she had to say! And I knew that I was as strong as she was."

"You were still stupid!"

"I was trying to be loyal and—"

"Okay, so you were loyal—and stupid. Harry's gun was a surprise. Roxanne could have carried one, too. You were incredibly stupid!" he said.

Okay, so he had a point. Still, the warmth of his touch seemed to take away the sting of the words.

"Thanks!" she told him. Then she shivered. "Oh, Justin, thank God you found me—"

"Thank God I found you, too, you stupid little fool."

"How did you—"

"I chased Harry's car on foot, until I saw the ruts in the snow turning into the woods here. And then I found where he'd left his car."

His fingers were shaking as he smoothed a stray lock of hair from her forehead.

She caught his hand. "You're bleeding!"

"Am I? I fell down at one point."

"Oh, Justin!"

"My hands are okay, Kristin. He had you here by the time I caught up with him. Then I was trying to be damned careful. I was so grateful that you were alive! I heard the last of what he said. Heard him confess to killing Myra. I was still wondering what was the best way to save you. Then I saw him pull the gun. The only thing I could think of to do was draw his fire until I could get around behind him, or at least to his side. It bought me the few seconds that I needed."

"And *I'm* stupid? You invited a bullet," she said with quiet reproach.

"I know these woods. And how to move in them. I was pretty sure of what I was doing."

"He nearly scared me to death!" Kristin murmured.

"He meant to murder you to death!" Justin said grimly, his arms tightening as he walked her across the snow. She could just hear a siren. The sheriff had reached them. He drove through the snow right into the copse.

"Hi, Bill!" Justin called. He indicated the path that he and Kristin had just taken through the snow. "Our killer is that way. I think he's still out."

"Are you both all right? You okay, Ms. Kennedy?" the sheriff called to her.

"Yes, I'm fine, thank you!" Kristin said.

"She's not fine at all. He almost strangled her," Justin said gruffly. "Sheriff, there's a lot to tell you, but maybe it can wait."

"I already got a lot from that Mr. Jones," the sheriff said. He cleared his throat. "I'm glad, Justin. I can't say that I always believed in you, but I did always like you, and I'm—well, I'm glad."

He tilted his head and walked on by them.

Still holding Kristin tightly in his arms, Justin walked over to the sheriff's Jeep and leaned against it.

"At least he asked me how I was," Kristin murmured. She looked up at Justin. His eyes were fiercely blue. "I am all right. You can put me down now."

"I know how you are," Justin said, and he shook his head slowly. "And now, I'm keeping you like this until we get you to the hospital."

"The hospital!"

"Umm. Your throat is black and blue. Kristin, he nearly did strangle you. And you're freezing. You need a night of observation."

"But—"

"Just overnight," Justin said. "And I'll be with you. I won't leave you. I promise."

He grinned. "I'll never leave you anywhere again. You don't stay where you're left, do you know that?"

She smiled. And she rested her head against his chest.

It wasn't what she wanted from him.

But it was a very nice start.

He didn't leave her.

The hospital was more of an ordeal than she had been expecting, but Justin was determined that she needed to be there. After she had been checked and poked and prodded, Roger and Sue were let in to see her, too.

It was nice, because she felt so very cared for, and because for once she and Justin were on the very best of terms before Roger and Sue.

When Roger and Sue were certain that Kristin was going to be fine, they were determined to leave. Justin gave them the keys to his house, asking them to make sure his uninvited guests got out again all right.

"I won't be home until morning. I'm keeping my eyes on this one. She'll probably try to walk home if I don't keep her here."

"Right," Roger agreed. He stared sternly at Kristin, reminding her that she was in trouble with him, too.

"Make yourselves at home," Justin told them, winking.

The two left hand in hand. Kristin wanted to talk. She couldn't. Nurses kept coming in and out.

She fell asleep.

When she woke in the morning, Justin was staring at her. She flushed, wondering what she looked like in the hospital gown, her hair a mess, no makeup. Well, he'd seen her a mess before.

"How are you feeling?" he asked her.

"Fine. Honestly. I feel fine."

"Good." He studied her closely, lifting her hair, then delicately placing a kiss at her nape. "You won't believe this, but the bruises have already almost faded. I'll step out. The doctor is going to come in and release you."

He left for the few moments it took for the doctor to give her a once-over and pronounce that she was, indeed, fine.

Then Justin was back with a shopping bag Sue had brought filled with some clothing and her toilet articles. He sat at the foot of the bed while she showered and dressed, and when she came out of the bathroom, he was still there. He reached for her hands.

"I thought you were in a hurry to take me home."

He shook his head solemnly. "I'm never taking you home again."

"What—?"

"You don't stay there when I take you. I've figured it out. I'm going to marry you. That way, when I take you home, you're with me. And I can always keep an eye on you."

"What?"

He smiled. "I love you, Kristin. But you know that, don't you? I love you desperately, and I'm in love with you, and I want to take you home with me for the rest of my life. Will you marry me?"

She started to fling her arms around him and kiss him. And then she pulled back.

"You were supposed to crawl and grovel your way through the snow."

"I know." He winced. "I just don't grovel well. I am sorry for ever doubting you, though. I'll never do so again. I swear it."

He kissed her, very tenderly. "You never, never doubted me," he said huskily.

"Oh, Justin, I do love you!" she told him.

And she kissed him back. And kissing him was so wonderful that she could have done it forever. She could have just leaned back and let it go on and on....

On a hospital bed.

She straightened. "Justin! I've got to tell Roger and Sue. Please. Right away, do you mind?"

He shook his head wryly. "Can't stay here anyway, I guess."

On the long drive back to his house, she sat next to him, and his arm was around her. She was amazed when he said that he'd move to Boston for her.

She knew what his home meant to him.

"Well," she said huskily, "I am growing rather fond of the country myself."

His arm came around her. He pulled her tight against him, and something about the feel of him then was far better than any five-mile crawl through the snow that he might have made.

When they reached his house she flew out of the car to ring the bell and bang on the door.

Roger answered it, his hair wild, his eyes wide. Kristin ignored him, bursting through the door. Sue wasn't in the living room.

She ran on through to the patio.

The table out there was set for two with crystal and china. Roger had been making mimosas with orange juice and champagne.

Soft music was playing....

And Sue was sitting there in an elegant bathrobe.

"Oh!" Kristin murmured.

"You're really early," Sue said nervously. "Kristin, it's barely seven."

"Oh, it's just that I had to tell you...."

"What?" Roger asked politely.

Justin was standing behind him. Kristin went running to him, throwing her arms around him. "We're getting married," she announced.

"That's wonderful!" Roger said.

"Kristin!" Sue leaped up.

And then they were all kissing and hugging one another.

Until Kristin wound up in Justin's arms again. And he held her, and she just looked into his eyes.

"I love you so much!" he whispered.

Roger was putting on his shirt. Sue slipped into her shoes.

Kristin managed to pull her eyes away from Justin's. "Oh, listen, you two, we're sorry. We'll leave—"

"No, no thanks," Roger said. "Sue and I will just go home. Our own little bedroom is starting to look like fantasy land. Well, at least it isn't Grand Central Station."

Sue gathered her things and followed her husband. "Breakfast is ready," she said to Justin and Kristin. "Mimosas are made . . . there are cushions on the floor, the pool water is nice and warm . . . well, goodbye. We'll see you tonight, all right? Dinner out somewhere. If you two can handle it."

"I'm sure we can," Kristin said demurely.

Sue and Roger left them. Kristin heard the front door close.

Justin smiled at her. "I love you so much, Kristin. You're everything that I ceased to believe in. You've given me back everything."

Kristin stood on her toes. She kissed his lips softly.

"The water is nice and warm," she murmured. "The mimosas are made."

"It shouldn't be wasted. Somebody really should have some nice, hot, wonderful, passionate sex, right?"

"Hey," Kristin said, laughing huskily, "that sure sounds right to me."

He swept her up into his arms. And kissed her.

And kissed her...

There was no reason to stop now.

No reason at all.

* * * * *

SILHOUETTE·INTIMATE·MOMENTS™

IT'S TIME TO MEET
THE MARSHALLS!

In 1986, bestselling author Kristin James wrote A VERY SPECIAL FAVOR for the Silhouette Intimate Moments line. Hero Adam Marshall quickly became a reader favorite, and ever since then, readers have been asking for the stories of his two brothers, Tag and James. At last your prayers have been answered!

In June, look for Tag's story, SALT OF THE EARTH (IM #385). Then skip a month and look for THE LETTER OF THE LAW (IM #393—August), starring James Marshall. And, as our very special favor to you, we'll be reprinting A VERY SPECIAL FAVOR this September. Look for it in special displays wherever you buy books.

MARSH-1

Silhouette Books®

You'll flip . . . your pages won't!
Read paperbacks *hands-free* with

Book Mate · I

The perfect "mate" for all your romance paperbacks

Traveling • Vacationing • At Work • In Bed • Studying • Cooking • Eating

Perfect size for all standard paperbacks, this wonderful invention makes reading a pure pleasure! Ingenious design holds paperback books OPEN and FLAT so even wind can't ruffle pages—leaves your hands free to do other things. Reinforced, wipe-clean vinyl-covered holder flexes to let you turn pages without undoing the strap...supports paperbacks so well, they have the strength of hardcovers!

Pages turn WITHOUT opening the strap

SEE-THROUGH STRAP

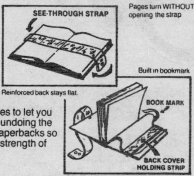

Reinforced back stays flat.

Built in bookmark

BOOK MARK

BACK COVER HOLDING STRIP

10" x 7¼", opened.
Snaps closed for easy carrying, too.

Available now. Send your name, address, and zip code, along with a check or money order for just $5.95 + .75¢ for delivery (for a total of $6.70) payable to Reader Service to:

Reader Service
Bookmate Offer
3010 Walden Avenue
P.O. Box 1396
Buffalo, N.Y. 14269-1396

Offer not available in Canada
*New York residents add appropriate sales tax.

BM-GR

PUT SOME SIZZLE INTO YOUR SUMMER WITH

SILHOUETTE SUMMER
Sizzlers
1991

Heading your way this summer are three sensual and romantic stories by these award-winning authors:

Kathleen Eagle
Marilyn Pappano
Patricia Gardner Evans

Sit back, bask in the sun and celebrate summer with this special collection of stories about three college roommates who rekindle their friendship—and discover love.

Available in June at your favorite retail outlets.

SIZZ